THE BOOKS OF

ELIZABETH BOWEN

NOVELS

A WORLD OF LOVE (1955)
THE LAST SEPTEMBER (1929, 1952)
THE HEAT OF THE DAY (1949)
THE DEATH OF THE HEART (1939)
THE HOUSE IN PARIS (1936)
TO THE NORTH (1933)

SHORT STORIES

EARLY STORIES (1951)
IVY GRIPPED THE STEPS (1946)
LOOK AT ALL THOSE ROSES (1941)

NON-FICTION

THE SHELBOURNE HOTEL (1951)
COLLECTED IMPRESSIONS (1950)
BOWEN'S COURT (1942)

THESE ARE *Borzoi Books* PUBLISHED IN NEW YORK BY

ALFRED A. KNOPF

A WORLD OF LOVE

A World of Love

Elizabeth Bowen

1955

Alfred A. Knopf NEW YORK

L. C. CATALOG CARD NUMBER: 55–5209

©ELIZABETH BOWEN, 1954

THIS IS A BORZOI BOOK,
PUBLISHED BY ALFRED A. KNOPF, INC.

COPYRIGHT *1954* by ELIZABETH BOWEN. *All rights reserved. No part of this book may be reproduced in any form without permission in writing from the publisher, except by a reviewer who may quote brief passages in a review to be printed in a magazine or newspaper. Manufactured in the United States of America. Published simultaneously in Canada by McClelland & Stewart Limited.*

FIRST EDITION

UNIVERSITY LIBRARY
UNIVERSITY OF ALBERTA

TO

CATHERINE POMEROY COLLINS

There is in us a world of Love to somewhat, though we know not what in the world that should be. . . . Do you not feel yourself drawn by the expectation and desire of some Great Thing?

Centuries of Meditations

A WORLD OF LOVE

I

THE sun rose on a landscape still pale with the heat
of the day before. There was no haze, but a sort of cop-
pery burnish out of the air lit on flowing fields, rocks,
the face of the one house, and the cliff of limestone over-
hanging the river. The river gorge cut deep through the
uplands. This light at this hour, so unfamiliar, brought
into being a new world—painted, expectant, empty, intense. The month was June, of a summer almost unknown; for this was a country accustomed to late waken-
ings, to daybreaks humid and overcast. At all times open
and great with distance, the land this morning seemed
to enlarge again, throwing the mountains back almost
out of view in the south of Ireland's amazement at being
cloudless.

Out in front of the house, on a rise of rough grass,
somewhat surprisingly stood an obelisk; which, now out-
lined by the risen sun, cast towards Montefort its long
shadow—only this connected the lordly monument with

3

the dwelling. For the small mansion had an air of having gone down: for one thing, trees had been felled around it, leaving space impoverished and the long low roofline framed by too much sky. The door no longer knew hospitality; moss obliterated the sweep for the turning carriage; the avenue lived on as a rutted track, and a poor fence, close up to the house, served to keep back wandering grazing cattle. Had the façade not carried a ghost of style, Montefort would have looked, as it almost did, like nothing more than the annex of its farm buildings—whose slipshod gables and leaning sheds, flaking whitewash and sagging rusty doors made a patchwork for some way out behind. A stone archway, leading through to the stables and nobly canopied by a chestnut tree, sprang from the side of the house and was still imposing.

Montefort stood at a right-angle to the near-by gorge, towards which it presented a blind end—though in this the vestige of a sealed-up Venetian window was to be traced. In its day the window had overlooked the garden which, broken-walled, still projected over the river view. A way zigzagged steeply down through thickets and undergrowth to the water's edge: the cliff arose from the water, opposite.

The half-asleep face of Montefort was at this hour drowned in early light.

· · ·

A GIRL came out of the house, and let herself through the gate in the fence. Wearing a trailing Edwardian muslin dress, she stepped out slowly towards the obelisk, shading her eyes. She walked first up the shadow, then round the base of the monument: this bore no inscription and had been polished only by rubbing cattle, whose hoofs had left a bald-trodden circle in the grass. Having come to a standstill, she drew a breath, propped an elbow on a convenient ledge of the stone, and, leaning, began to re-read a letter; or, rather, ponder over what she more than half seemed to know by heart. Afterwards, refolding the letter, she took a long look round at all the country, as though following one deep draught up with one of another kind. Kindled by summer though cool by nature, she was a beauty. The cut of her easy golden hair was anachronistic over the dress she wore: this, her height, and something half naïve half studied about her management of the sleeves and skirts made her like a boy actor in woman's clothes, while what was classical in her grace made her appear to belong to some other time. Her brows were wide, her eyes an unshadowed blue, her mouth more inclined to smile than in any other way to say very much—it was a face perfectly ready to be a woman's, but not yet so, even in its transcendency this morning. She was called Jane and was twenty years old. All at once, stepping clear of the obelisk, she looked intently back at the house behind her, and in particular at two adjoining windows in the top storey. Across those, however, curtains were still drawn.

INSIDE the room, in the mantled claret-red dusk, nothing was in movement except the bluebottle now bumping buzzing against the ceiling. Here or there, sun spattered the carpet, rents in the curtains let through what were to be when the sleeper woke shafts of a brightness quite insupportable. The fourposter, of a frame immense, was overdraped with more of the damask stuff: at one side the hangings were tucked back to allow access to things on the bedside table—a packet of Gold Flake, a Bible, a glass with dregs, matches, sunglasses, sleeping pills, a nail file, and a candlestick caked with wax into which the finished wick had subsided. A damaged Crown Derby saucer held strawberry stalks, cigarette stubs, ash: some uneaten strawberries sweetly tainted the already unfresh surrounding air. The bedend had during the night become a cascade of twisted rejected blankets; feather pillows too had been flung away—triumphant the sleeper now lay dead flat, flat out. A sheet traced the declivities of her body; her upturned face seemed to be sealed by the resolution never, if so it might be, to wake at all.

But the door opened; a step caught a creaking floorboard. A big blonde woman inched herself in, then halted, with a look at once of uncertainty and affront. "Oh, then you're still asleep," she at last said. The door swung and clicked on its latch behind her, and though she jumpily gave it a backward glance she seemed glad to have the decision made—advancing further into the room, she began to pick feathers from the carpet, sighing and supporting her bust with one arm. Having thus arrived near the dressing-table, she straightened up, put back some wisps of hair in front of the glass, and, as though egged on by her reflection, more loudly said: "I said, so you're still asleep."

The other woman shuddered from top to toe, then started to strangle with morning coughing. She reared her head up blindly, finished the bout, then flopped back again, instinctively dragging with her a bed-curtain which she wound round her in a tent, in whose depths she vainly tried to submerge. Giving up, she asked in a charnel tone: "What is it?"

"What o'clock, do you mean?"

"No. What do you want?"

"I wondered if Jane was in here."

"Is she?"

"No. So I've no idea where she's gone. However, it was only that Fred keeps asking.—Did you know your pillow was shedding, one of your pillows? I wonder which."

"Then do take the whole bang lot away!—No, not *now!*" (for the other approached the bed) "Later on, Lilia, for heaven's sake!"

Lilia continued, however, to search the lair with her large blue heavily vacant eyes. "And how are you this morning?" she asked unhopefully.

"Oh, fresh as a daisy, thank you—as you can see."

"Oh."

"And you?" reluctantly croaked the other.

"After yesterday, how can you ask, Antonia?"

"What happened yesterday?"

"The Fête."

"So it did. So you mean now you're dead."

"In this heat how can I know what I am? Merely that Fête was the last straw—oh, imagine having to go to that! After those shoes also my feet are torture; but chiefly it is this everlasting buzzing inside my head, not to speak of waking drenching with perspiration. And in this heat this house gets more dreadful day after day. However—" Lilia turned her attention to the bedside table. "It looks to me," she said in a brisker tone, "as though you'd again gone to sleep with your candle burning. Only look at it. Did you?"

"I've no idea."

"I lie sleepless, sometimes, picturing you in flames.— Done with this glass, have you?"

"If it's empty."

"Then I think I might as well take it down. And this fruit seems to have started bringing in flies." Lilia reached for the glass, then for the saucer, then was struck by a thought. "But now that leaves you nowhere for your ash. I know what I'll do, I'll send Maud up with another."

"No, don't do that, Lilia! Don't let Maud in!"

"Maud has come out in hives."

"Not Jane too, I hope?"

"The child over-ate at the Fête, then brought home more. You never ought to have given her that money.— No, I said, I haven't seen Jane this morning, any more than anyone else seems to have done. As I said, that's why Fred's in a state—it seems she yesterday said she'd be sure to go out with him to his hay this morning. He can't or won't believe she could break a promise. 'Well, I'm sorry for you,' I said, 'but what ever do you expect after that Fête and staying there late dancing?' However, no, she's not asleep in her room.—Now you *are* awake, I suppose you will want your tea?"

"In a minute, if it could come up calmly."

"Come up what?"

"Never mind."

"Well, I do mind, because I heard what you said. I can only say I am doing more than I can, night and day attempting always to have this, that, and the other the way you want it, and if you're still not satisfied I am sorry. No one would be gladder than I would if things ran smoothly, but if *you* had ever attempted to keep this old terrible house, you would just see. Do you think I for a moment ever forget you have every right to be satisfied when you choose to come here? What upsets me is—"

"*Lilia! Not* at this hour!"

"You don't yet even know what o'clock it is."

"I do know it's not the o'clock for this."

"Oh, very well," replied Lilia. "By all means. Just as you like." She added the candlestick to the glass and saucer and, keeping the pyramid they formed in precarious balance against her bosom, proceeded through the tricky dusk to the door—her form, the exhausted mauve of her cotton dress, by turns appearing opaque or ghostly. She was electing to move, as she sometimes did, with a sort of superior smoothness, as though trollied. Antonia lay watching suspiciously, then shot up. "Hi, stop! You're not taking away my matches?"

This caused a halt, once again on the creaking board. "As I never touch anything without first asking, your matches should be where they were. Aren't they?"

"No idea where they were."

"If you want to know, I can see them even from here." Lilia shifted her burden, set her right arm free, and with it majestically pointed. The arm—white, soft-skinned, still remarkably shapely—stayed outstretched, with unquivering forefinger, while Antonia, scuffling around the curtain, came on the matchbox, shook it, and relapsed with a grunt.—"Quite right. Oh, thank you. So sorry."

"Will that be all?"

Antonia, lighting a cigarette, sent a glance after the closing door.

L I L I A, wife of Fred Danby, mother of Jane and Maud, was half the hostess at Montefort, half not. There were times—of which this morning was one—when she felt either galled or weighed upon by the ambiguity. The fact was that Antonia owned the place, which had come to her upon the death of a cousin, and that the Danbys' status here was uncertain, never secure, never defined. They were not her tenants, for they paid no rent; neither were they her caretakers, for they drew no salary. Fred farmed the land, and paid across to Antonia a half share of such profits as could be made; he and his family lived in the house for nothing, the best room in it being kept for Antonia to occupy when and how she chose. Of this arrangement it had not yet been decided whether it did or did not work, still less if it were equitable or, if not so, not so at whose expense. One could only say it had lasted for twenty-one years, owing perhaps partly to all parties' reluctance to sitting down and having anything out, or to binding themselves to anything hard-and-fast, or to thinking out anything better. Antonia shrank from bother; Fred worked too hard to have time for more, and Lilia's brooding attitude was ambivalent—she disliked Montefort, wilted under the life here, but had ceased to more than dream of escape. As she saw it, here were herself and Fred kept dangling upon Antonia's caprices; as against which, here was their patroness yearly drifting more into their debt and power. If the Danbys were to walk out—though indeed, to where?—Antonia would have to grapple with the decision she had so far staved off: whether to part with Montefort or to take it over. Her overweening sentiment for the place went, as her cousin's had done before her, with neither wish nor ability to remain here always. Her visits were sudden and on the whole far apart; being more and more timed, of later years, to coincide with Jane's returns home. The cost of Jane's education —first at expensive boarding school, then abroad, lately at a select London secretarial college—had been met by Antonia: who knew how? Jane could now be held to be qualified for her first post: what it should be or when she should take it up was not yet decided. . . . Maud, the second daughter, lived at home and attended the local Protestant school.

The relationship of the Danbys to Antonia was puzzling until one knew the story. Guy, one-time owner of

Montefort, Antonia's first cousin and dear ally, had, when he fell in battle early in 1918, been engaged to Lilia—at seventeen a wonderful golden willow of a girl. That enchanting love-on-a-leave, that idealization undoomed—as he probably knew—ever to fade, so far failed to connect in Guy with outside reality that he had forgotten to make a will. When he was killed, therefore, any money he had went, together with Montefort, to Antonia, who apart from anything else was his next of kin. The fiancée was left unprovided for. Antonia had felt this unfair, as it more than was. Unwilling to profit by Guy's oversight, she sought out Lilia, whom she had yet to meet. Lilia, already so dazed by Guy as to be only a shade more stupefied by his death, was indeed in a bad way—whirled by the courtship out of her natural sphere (suburbia merging into the Thames Valley), untrained to work and now not disposed to try, unfitted to take up life again with her own people, with whom Guy, it transpired, had made bad blood. Ill met, since this was the outcome, had Guy been by the ballroom-blue moonlight of Maidenhead. It was clear Lilia did not know where to turn. Had she been left alone, which she was not, life yet might have forced her on to her own feet: there could have been benefit, at this crisis, from a no more than discreet and limited aid. But Antonia had not known where to stop, and never had intervention proved more fatal. Instead of giving Lilia a sum down or

arranging to make her a fixed allowance, she had ended
by virtually adopting this girl of all but her own age.
Endlessly was she to involve herself with the incurably
negative destiny of this person: there she was, saddled
with Lilia for what looked like always. Pushed off into a
series of occupations, placed in vain in a series of gift
shops, tea shops, brought in vain to the notice of likely
friends, Lilia came bobbing back again like a thing on
water. Blight had cut short her early beauty, apathy
mildewed what might have remained, and her depend-
ence upon Antonia more and more went with a profound mistrust. Still worse, Antonia's unevenly curbed
dislike completed the demoralization Guy's heady love,
then speedy death, had begun. This had gone on till
Lilia was nearly thirty; when Antonia, at her wits' end,
had decided to marry her off to Fred.

Fred was Guy's and Antonia's illegitimate cousin, by-
blow son of roving Montefort uncle. As to his mother,
who vanished, little was known: it was generally held
she'd had foreign blood, to which Fred's colouring gave
support. He had been left in at Montefort, not reclaimed, and allowed to grow up in the stable yards, attempts to school him having been dropped in view of
his usefulness round the place. At fifteen, mature for his
age, he was said to be poaching salmon, going with
women—if he *was* wild, it was wildness sheathed in
stolidity. Few had encountered Fred: those who did so

liked him—there had been, on the whole, regret when
he cleared out. He walked out one morning without a
word to anyone, to be heard of some time afterwards in
Australia. The 1914 War saw him, one heard, at a battle-
front with the Australian army. Some years after that
war, when Montefort was closed and the lands let out,
Fred was reported about the country: Antonia tried to
contact him but found him again gone.

His next return had been a matter of fate. Antonia,
camping alone in Montefort, staring out of a window at
the June twilight, saw him sauntering down the rise
from the obelisk as though he had never been an hour
away. She hastened out, shouting: Fred came back indoors with her and they drank together. No, this time—
he informed her—he had no plans; he in fact would not
be half sorry if someone said to him he was back for
good. He had quite a mind to stay in the country if he
could see his way to it, but he doubted that. She, on her
side, was at a crisis of worry about the place—the feck-
lessness or ill-will of the grazing tenants, the decay getting a hold on the shut-up house. With a rush, on the
strength of a brain-flash, she brought out the proposi-
tion about Montefort. He put down his glass and turned
his head away slowly, as though offended: forbiddingly,
he advised her to think it over. Would *he* think it over?
Well, he supposed he might. He had then shoved past
her out of the darkening diningroom. That night, as

Antonia lay tense, excited, yet another comet shot through her brain: she could hardly wait to put up the idea to Fred. When next they met, in the yard next morning, she point-blank asked—had he got a wife? Fred's eye for a moment just flitted over her—no, he told her, after deliberation. That was fine, she exulted: all could now be straightforward. For, let her tell him, a woman went with the land. Take one, take both: in fact, it was both or neither.

"Would it be you?" he not unreasonably asked.

On learning it was to be Lilia, whose legend he surprisingly did recall, he said he saw no harm in taking a look. Lilia, summoned by telegram, unknowingly brought herself over from England on approval. She arrived flaccid after the all-night journey, debilitated by sea-sickness, quite her worst—she had not been sleeping; morbid blue virginal circles were round her eyes; her talk was exclusively of fatigues and worries. Fred came in as far as doorways, where he lingered taking oblique notice: after thirty-six hours he was able to intimate that as far as *he* went, the thing was on. Would Antonia speak to the lady on his behalf?

Lilia, on being told she was asked in marriage, incontrovertibly answered that Fred was common. "You would not even ask me to think of this," she added, "if it was not that you're sick of the sight of me. So this is what it has come to! Have you forgotten how once I was

good enough for Guy? It would have been better, I
now see, if I had thrown myself off that ship on the way
over. I all but did, let me tell you. When that telegram
came, I knew you had something up your sleeve."

"To me, you know, Fred's an attractive man."

"Then why don't you have him?"

"Because I don't want him," flashed out Antonia
thoughtlessly.

"*I* see. So you put him up to this?"

"But don't you want a home?—my heavens! Don't
you ever want children? They'd be as pretty as posters:
you wait and see!"

"After all these years, you think of that."

"The occasion didn't arise till now."

"You think so? Thank you," Lilia coldly returned.
"How many other offers do you imagine I might not
have always had, if I had chosen to lift a finger, instead
of staying faithful to Guy's memory? That, of course,
you never would understand."

That brought a clashing silence, a contemptuously
brutal stare from Antonia under which Lilia folded up
—she sobbed and began to pluck at her handkerchief.
"Home where?" she asked, with an air of shame. "What
sort of home could *he* ever give me?" She glanced round
the crouching room with its smoky ceiling, then through
the window at the void skyline. "Antonia, you and he
can't mean *here?*"

"Where else?"

"But this is a dreadful house."

"It was Guy's. He loved it."

"He seldom spoke of it."

"Seldom to you, perhaps."

"I could never care for a place I could not keep nice."

"Once you're married, you'll find you'll be twice the girl!"

An authentic shudder ran through Lilia's frame. "I could never, now, embark upon all *that*."

"Rats! Try."

"Oh, you are sometimes terrible!"

"Well, there you are," said Antonia. "Think it over—only don't shillyshally; it wouldn't be fair to Fred. By all means go back to the tea shop if you'd rather; but if you do, this time you must stick it out—or find something else for yourself. I shan't be able to prop you up any longer: the point has come when I won't, so you'll have to face it. I'm sick of having Montefort run to ruin; I'm going into this partnership with Fred; we'll need all I have to patch up and stock the place. So you, I'm afraid, must be left to your own resources—which of course may be endless, for all I know!"

"For all you care," Lilia said in a dead voice.

She had remained for three days stunned by the ulti-matum, shocked by the outrage, mindless with indeci-sion; while Fred, appearing only at meals, stole at her

glances in which respect, pity, and increasing desire were
to be felt to merge. Aware of, slowly worked upon by
those glances, she still refused to address Fred or meet
his eyes. At last she capitulated; and, as Antonia could
not now wait to be off to London, the wedding went
through almost at once. Having escorted the couple
home from the church, Antonia leaped back into the
beribboned hackney and made her habitual dash to the
boat train. She looked behind her once—they still stood
framed in the doorway, blankly watching her go. They
put no face on the thing.

It is not known what words Fred and Lilia then or in
the following time exchanged. Left there to mate, they
mated; but that is never all. Unleashed by marriage, his
unforeseen passion for her ran its unspeaking course,
just outlasting the birth of their first child, Jane. Antonia, returning to Montefort into the thick of that, was
aghast. Though after all, she said to herself, why not?
All the same, something monstrous seemed to her to be
under her own roof. These two engendered a climate;
the air round them felt to her sultry, over-intensified,
strange: one could barely breathe it. Yes, they had
passed beyond her—she had made the match, they the
marriage. For Lilia that was an epoch, not to occur
again, of ascendancy over her former patron. She was
again in beauty, of a lofty late lightless inert kind; her
pregnancy added to and became her, and this great,

never quite smiling snow-woman, come into being almost overnight, was formidable. She neutrally and abstractedly eyed Antonia, heard her speak or spoke to her from a distance—she was queening it, and, which was still worse, queening it naturally, unawares. Smug, thought Antonia, cutting that visit short.

That, however, had been twenty years ago. When next Antonia came to Montefort Jane was an infant, and Fred's kind, unfailing patience with Lilia confirmed the rumours that he was off again, back to his loves in the lanes. It was when Jane took form as herself that her father entered upon his first and last, devouring, hopeless, and only love.

FRED had not, in reality, this June morning, more than once asked where Jane was—upon there seeming to be no answer, he had turned and gone out without a word more. Now, an hour later, he had looked in again: here he was, standing in the kitchen, hastily drinking out of a thick Delft cup. Lilia, coming down from Antonia's room, found him with Kathie, the little servant, at his elbow, waiting to spoon more sugar into the tea when he should pause. Fred's shirt was open, showing the matted black hair, here and there glistening with tea drops, on his barrel chest. He now was a thickset man, about fifty-three, with a touch of the Latin about his pigmentation and cast of features. His skull was broad, with forehead receding somewhat; his muscle-webbed neck was short. His far-apart, dark, and prominent eyes were inhabited by a look of curious patience, as though he had at one time been struck across them and might be so again. Grey streaked his short, unevenly clipped moustache, though not yet the hair plastered flat to his head.

He bumped down the empty cup on the table and, the heat of the tea coming out in sweat, pulled a khaki handkerchief from his breeches pocket and mopped round his face and behind his ears. Kathie nipped to refill the cup, but he shook his head. Seeing Lilia come in, with, perhaps, news, he could not refrain from one glance of hope; she, however, only went straight to put down the glass, saucer, and candlestick on the already cluttered board of the sink. After that, subsiding on to a chair, she went on taking pleasure in saying nothing, till he caught her eye by making as though to go. She then asked: "Know there's a fly on your neck?"

To oblige, he slapped at it, but in the wrong place.

"Oh, well," she yawned, "keep it, if you prefer it. I should break down if one walked on *me*. I too well remember where they have come from. Going out again now, are you?"

"Mm-mm. Why?"

"Then what were you waiting for?"

"Swallow my tea," said Fred. He made for the door.

"Oh, about Jane," said Lilia, slowly turning her head. Like a fool he stopped in his course, to hear. His wife went on: "Well, she was not up there."

"Up where?" he asked apparently vaguely, plucking away at an old nail loose in the lintel of the door.

"Not up there with Antonia, for a wonder."

No more was necessary: Fred was gone. "He's scalded for time," remarked Kathie, through one then another window watching him cross the yard; she brought the candlestick to the middle table and began to jab at the wax in it with a broken knife. Lilia looked on at the process with a gathering frown. "It's extraordinary, Kathie," she said at last, "how you always do what need not be done immediately. Look at those dishes over from last evening, only attracting flies into the sink; and where do I see Miss Antonia's tea-tray, now she's awake?"

Kathie willingly scrubbed her hands on her apron and made a dart for the cupboard of better china. Searching about for unchipped pieces, she volunteered: "I'm half sure I saw Miss Jane this morning, away out over the country in a ball gown."

"Then why not say so?"

"Away out over, and I'd the sun in my eyes.—Unless could it ever have been a Vision?"

"Now don't *you* start being peculiar, in this heat.— Ball gown? There's no such thing in this house. Miss

Jane leaves her fashionable clothes in London, and what
should *I* do with a ball gown, I'd like to know?"

"I'd like to know!" echoed Kathie, nonplussed. She
gave two bangs to a tray, to dislodge crumbs, took a cloth
to a smear, then devoutly began to set out Antonia's tea-
things. Through the propped-open windows, the door
ajar, came in the sound of the tractor three fields away—
they were hay-cutting early, this dewless morning. The
mechanical hum was louder because of the stillness
around the house—not a rustle anywhere; the usual
murmurs of summer were suspended. Not a breath travelled over these uplands under the mountains or fanned
its way down the river gorge: the heat stood over the land
like a white-hot sword, causing an apprehensive hush.
Here in the kitchen the strips of flypaper hung from the
ceiling without swaying. What was eerie was that a snow-
like reflection came in from the sunstruck white buildings across the yard.

The green of the ivy over the window-bars and the
persisting humidity of the stone-flagged floors made the
kitchen look cool without being so. This was the room
in Montefort which had changed least; routine abode in
its air like an old spell. Generations of odours of baking
and basting, stewing and skimming had been absorbed
into the limewashed walls, leaving wood ash, raked cin-
ders, tea leaves, wrung-out cloths, and lamp oil freshly
predominant. The massive table, on which jigs had been

danced at the harvest homes, was probably stronger than, now, the frame of the house—today's slops and stains superficially lay on the bleach from years of scrubbing; the grain of the wood was dinted by chopper-blows. The great and ravenous range, of which no one now knew how to quell the roaring, was built back into a blackened cave of its own—on its top, a perpetual kettle sent out a havering thread of steam, tea stewed in a pot all day, and the lid heaved, sank on one or another of the jostling pots, saucepans, and cauldrons. Mush for the chickens, if nothing else, was never not in the course of cooking. Also, the range remained Montefort's sole means of heating water; none of the innovations—boilers, plumbing, and so on—envisaged once by Antonia had been yet installed, nor did it seem probable that they would be. There was not the money. The sink's one tap connected with a rainwater tank which had run dry—since then a donkey cart with a barrel rattled its way daily down to the river pool. Drinking water came from the spring near by—a crock with a dipper lived under the Delft-crowded dresser between the windows. On the dresser, from one of the hooks for cups, hung a still handsome calendar for the year before; and shreds of another, previous to that, remained tacked to the shutter over the sink. These, with the disregarded dawdling and often stopping of the cheap scarlet clock wedged in somewhere between the bowls and dishes, spoke of the almost total irrelevance of Time, in the abstract, to this ceaseless kitchen. One arrived, at the most, by instinct, guesswork, or calculation at which day of the week it ought to be or perhaps was. What had to be done in here was to be done only at its own pace, always lagging behind a little in the race with necessity. Something was always wanted but not ready.

Outdoors, the farm ran by the watch strapped inexorably to Fred's wrist. As master he had the name of being a terror, throwing out what he detected to be a slack man as soon as look at him; but as against that, he had been bred here and knew fundamentally what he was working with: men he chose to keep chose to stay— it was recognized that himself was the one he drove hardest of all. Inside Montefort, it was only Maud who ever shook or poked at the defective clock or ran round plaguing to know what the time could be. The child worshipped Big Ben, and how was she to hear the ether quiver with His strokes if she knew not when to tune in on her battery set?

Maud's summer holidays had begun.

Now Kathie started for upstairs with Antonia's tea, and Lilia seized the occasion to kick her shoes off—they were white canvas, high-heeled, a little grubby. Antonia had given her espadrilles, but she never would sink so low. Her feet, though today swollen, were pretty, and sizes smaller than Jane's: in winters only, when left alone with Fred, did she flap about all day in her chicken boots. She leaned back, easing herself on the wooden chair, in almost an ecstasy of lassitude. Bust arched up, arms falling slackly down, she drove thoughts off and forgot flies; she was prepared to consider, though not yet, her next move in the unequal battle with the day. She was not long alone, however, for Maud came in— the child, last heard of going off to the river, had somehow got back into the house; and evidently this was to be one of her days for elaborately stalking about on tiptoe, gnawing her lips with the effort to make no sound. Ignoring Lilia—whose willingness not to see her more than matched her wish not to be seen—Maud made direct for the kitchen dresser, where she took a pin from a cup, an egg from a bowl. She could have got out again, always with nothing said, had a crisis of violent itching not come upon her: standing where she was, she had to scratch one bare leg, in furious motion, with a loud skinny rasping, against the other. Lilia was so far roused as to turn and stare moodily at her second daughter.

"What are you doing with that egg?"

"Taking it."

"How am I to know how many there are? And it's disgusting, keeping on sucking them like a serpent."

"Why?"

"And overheating your blood, with Cousin Antonia unable to stand the sight of you as it is."

Maud's high forehead, exposed by the skinning-back of her hair, was indeed lumpy with crimson hives. She was twelve years old. Short plaits were strained round her skull to meet at the top, secured by a limp but precise bow of tartan ribbon. Her cotton frock with its pattern of orange horses had shrunk in the wash and clung to her narrow chest—it was clean but for some ghostly fruit-stains from the summer before. Maud was the neatest person about the house. In view of all that she was and did, there was something unfair, confounding, about her air of propriety—caught out, one might have considered, by developing spots, she carried these with nonchalance, even hauteur. Having been occupied, while her mother spoke, in expertly pricking both ends of the egg, she returned the pin to the cup and looked round the kitchen. Lilia by reflex compressed her toes, as though to appear to have shoes on; but it was upon the candlestick that Maud's eye lit; the child advanced to the table, put down the egg, and began to scoop up the chipped-off drippings.

Lilia said: "What are you doing messing with that wax?"

"I need it."

"Leave it, I tell you!"

"What, to be thrown away?" Maud stood working the wax to a ball between the palms of her hands. She pointed out: "It's useful for images."

"Why aren't you out of doors?"

"Where's Kathie?"

"Never you mind. Go out. But keep in the shade."

"I am in the shade in here."

"Argue, argue, argue," Lilia returned, abstractedly—for, what kept Kathie so long in Antonia's room? Maud dropped the wax into her pocket, picked up the egg, looked once again round the kitchen, decided to go, so went. Kathie, at last, could be heard pegging down the stairs.

KATHIE had left the curtains still undisturbed. Antonia finished her cup of tea, groaned, ground a cigarette into the saucer, and lay back, with again the idea of sleep. Jane chose this moment to enter; Antonia, equally, chose to fail to bring the girl in the sunny dusk into focus. There was therefore a pause, during which Jane vaguely stood at the bed's foot. "Well, come round," said Antonia finally. "I can't see you. Oh, so that is the ball dress?"

Jane, crestfallen, cried: "Then you're not surprised?"

"You were seen."

"Someone's been in, then, already? Somebody told you?" There sat the morning tray, sad confirmation.

"Half the world has been in," stated Antonia.

"Which of them saw me?"

"Kathie."

"Oh, that's all right.—Not that it *is* a ball dress," Jane went on, touching the high throat, flopping an angel sleeve.

Antonia, after a hostile yawn, said: "Well, another beautiful day?"

"*I* think so," the girl gently asserted.

"You do? Then suppose you tell me, we shall be doing —what?"

"Oh, I expect there'll be something to do, Antonia."

"Nerve-racking ghastly endless sublime weather! No, I can't simply live in it, can't take it. What's it meant for? Something has got to happen."

Jane flashed on Antonia a brimming, speaking look— lips apart, eyes meaning and startled. But then she seemed to retreat, so only said: "For instance, *I* put on this."

"So you did. Yes, I was wondering why."

"I get so sick of the sight of my arms and legs."

"That all it was?"

Jane parried: "What do I look like?"

"Where did it come from?"

"Simply out of a trunk. It must belong, I suppose, to somebody dead."

"Don't be too certain; it may have been mine!"

Jane coloured up for a moment, but then answered composedly: "No, surely you can't be as old as that." She trailed into closer view, seated herself on the bed's edge, turned her bust to show the antique cut of the bodice, invited Antonia to finger the fragile skirt. Antonia grumbled: "You may be right."

"Oh, you know I am. Also, smell it!" She bunched up and proffered a sort of bouquet of the yellowing stuff.

"Pah!" jibbed Antonia. "Musty. Take it away."

"Me to go away?"

"No, I never said that."

"Sachets, though, too, in the mustiness," Jane insisted. "One can know it was meant to be worn again."

"No, on the contrary—no, it had had its funeral. Delicious hour for somebody, packing away her youth. Last looks at it, pangs, perhaps tears even. Then, down with the lid!"

"What, does youth really end with a bang, like that?"

"It used to. Better if it still did."

Antonia, as so often, spoke into nothing—for Jane, not awaiting the answer to her idle question, had got up and gone to the looking-glass. There she stood, back turned to the bed, searching impersonally for the picture Antonia had failed to care to find—or for the meaning of the picture, without which there could be no picture at all. "What egotists the dead seem to be," she said. "This summery lovely muslin not to be worn again because *she* could not? Why not imagine me?" She stepped back on to a flounce of the hem, which tore.

"Who'd she have been?" she wondered, roping the fullness round her to see the damage. "One of your ancestors?"

"One of yours too, if so."

"Why, yes. Only I have the bar sinister."

"By the way, you forgot your father this morning."

"No!"

"So they say," said Antonia, still more amiably.

Fred's child's first blank then utterly stricken look, in reflection, was to be watched by the woman left behind on the bed; until Jane, suspecting this might be so, hurriedly bent over the dressing-table, to make a play of absorption in what was on it—disentangling pearls, puffing ash or powder off that or this. But the play broke down; nor could her burning forehead, towards the glass, be hidden by the forward fall of her hair. Failing to cover what she felt, she all the more exposed him to mocking pity—her hand shook, she knocked over a plastic bottle, caught a sleeve on the knob of an open drawer. She steadied herself. "But he's busy, out at the hay."

"Yes, by now, I daresay. But you kept him dangling about."

The bluebottle bumbled; Antonia lay; Jane stood. Antonia said suddenly, to the ceiling: "I'm not heartless, you know; only bad-hearted." She reached for her sunglasses, put them on, and sat up. "Must have more air.

Yes, you'll have to open the curtains." That relieved Jane—rings jangled back after each other along the rod; Antonia winced at the violence with which the gloom tore. Morning blazed fully into the littered room; pungent quivering heat from the roots of grass welled in over the sills of the open windows; the obelisk and the distance swam into view. Jane, after a look outdoors, was able to say tranquilly: "I forgot."

"It was not important to you."

The girl made a sort of denying movement, as though to say, no, *that* had really not been the case. Antonia poked at her packet of Gold Flake—yes, one left—then asked, with a sinister carelessness: "Who was there, last night?"

"At the dancing? Nobody you didn't see at the Fête."

"Oh."

"Why?"

Antonia flung the sheet back. "I shall get up."

"I'll go away, then?" the girl too readily said.

"If you call it going: you're all the time somewhere else. What's the matter with you? Why are you in this trance?"

"Am I?" Jane asked, with a touch of awe at herself.

"What have you been doing?"

"Reading a letter, only." Jane hesitated, put up a hand and glanced at it, as though wondering whether it should or should not have sealed her mouth. But she *was* glad to have spoken. "One of some letters," she said, beginning to smile.

"What, then the post's come? What have they done with mine?"

"Not the post. No, these came out of a trunk." Before more could follow, Jane with a few long steps had gone out, shutting the door behind her.

II

JANE, the evening before, had come home alone. The Fête, when darkness began to fall, reached its conclusion in outdoor dancing on the lawn of the castle which had been the scene all day; she like the other girls had stayed on, though not, like Kathie, up to the end. She left on an impulse. Music followed her over the empty country as she bicycled home through the lanes between there and Montefort; dust wraithlike rose from under her wheels. Honeysuckle sweetened the deepening hedges, from beyond which breathed distances cool with hay. The land had not yet composed itself quite to sleep, for light was not gone and might never go from the sky. The air through which she was swiftly passing was mauve, and tense with suspended dew: her own beautiful restlessness was everywhere.

From somewhere out behind Montefort she at one time imagined she heard a call; she unchained the gates and rode up the avenue. The house, nothing as she approached it but a black outline, was deserted—doors

34

and windows open, but not a lamp lit. Neither glad nor
sorry but mystified, and still with that inexplicable feeling of being summoned, she looked into all the rooms—
remains of supper were on a table: having come in, had
the others gone out again? She scarcely wondered. For
for her the house was great with something: she *had*
been sent for, and in haste. Why? Only attics now remained to be searched; and how could they (she reflected, for she was practical) show anything? She remembered at least a hat, not unlike Lady Latterly's of
this afternoon, left for years up there to hang on a
broken harp. She lighted a candle and went to look.

Of the stuffed, stuffy attics baking under the roof,
only one was inhabited—by Kathie. They were loftlike,
with here a pane let into the slates, there a floor-low window balked by the front parapet. The flame of Jane's
candle consumed age in the air; toppling, the wreckage
left by the past oppressed her—so much had been stacked
up and left to rot; everything was derelict, done for,
done with. Out of the dark projected cobwebby antlers
or the broken splendid legs of a chair: shocking was it to
her that there should be so much ignominy, perhaps
infamy. She took the hat quickly, knocking a twang
from the harp, and turned to go—she half thought a bat
stirred in the rafters. But no, no sound, nothing more at
all of that crepitation of opening leathery wings—there
was a stir, but within herself. Her halted shadow lay on

a trunk. She planted the candle on the floor, knelt down, and set about shifting albums, stacks of them, from the top. She unbuckled straps, put the lid back, and began to draw out the inexhaustible muslin of the dress; out of it, having been wedged in somewhere, tumbled the packet of letters. They fell at her feet, having found her rather than she them.

THE FAMILY knew no more than that Jane had come back and gone to bed—they supposed, tired. The home-coming rattle of her bicycle along the ruts of the avenue had been heard by Fred and Antonia, out strolling: they had glanced at one another and turned back, but nowhere was there a sign of her indoors. Lilia had, all the time, been lying silently in the dark on a sofa under a window when Jane passed through the drawingroom —in at one door, out again at the other. They all had been to the Fête, and a backwash from it still agitated their tempers and nerves—in the house itself residual pleasure-seeking ghosts had been set astir. The Hunt Fête, which drew the entire country, now was the sole festivity of the lonely year, for Montefort the annual outing—which, more and more each summer, required nerve. One does not go into the world and come home the same: isolation has altered its nature when one re-turns. Rare were sallies from Montefort—Fred grudged the time; Lilia, shy and huffy, felt unequal these days even to braving church (Maud had become the solitary, seldom-failing occupier of the family pew). As to the Fête, however, there remained an imperative: this challenging social gathering, which one paid money to enter, was a thing apart. The Danbys "appeared" at it as unfailingly as they could be relied upon to be nowhere else. There they were, still themselves, still alive; forgotten since this time last year, they had gone on existing, inside those gates knotted shut with a chain. Fred, wearing a cap, made one of the crowd watching the jumping; while his wife, fashionably got up, stood apart, at bay, high heels ground into the lawn. The lost lady suffered under wondering stares.

This time the Montefort party had gained by including Jane and Antonia. Jane, legging it round the place swinging a tray and in a small muslin apron, was among the busiest helpers at the tea tent; and Antonia had opened in good form—hatless, jewelled, flashing her black glasses, spotting friends, capping sentiments, barking greetings. Her age, able to be calculated to a day by the many present who still knew her, if anything added to her showing: each year made more of her, not less. The gorgeousness of her parrot-green satin shirt, stuffed into a skirt of inconspicuous flannel, somehow drew the eye from, by defying, her stumpy build: she was of high voltage, as is the case more often with short men than

little women—and indeed little she was not: her top
half suggested a greater stature, having breadth, poise,
carriage, imposing style. Stains on her long fine fingers,
actually nicotine, were with awe attributed to her pro-
fession—as an artist photographer she had made a name,
young; she still had the name, and was understood still
to be making money. So widely had she been heard of,
and for so long, that she arrived at having been heard of
even here: today she was playing her part of fame. Wherever she turned, she by turning flattered: the crowd
pleased her because she was pleasing it.

The Fête, dazzling concourse of marquees ringed
round a lawn, had as backdrop the stucco face of the
castle, a terrace along which urns blazed with geraniums,
a cascade of steps upon which the new English chatelaine
from time to time interestingly appeared. (It had been
during one of these sorties of Lady Latterly's that she
had perceived Jane, had her led up, chatted, noted her
name and even address in case of possible future need,
and in short taken a fancy to the girl.) The kaleidoscopic
shimmer over the Fête spun over and into the shadow of
glossy beeches, the cool of which encaved ice-cream
stalls; while from the mound overspread by a nightlike
cedar a handbell clanged or a megaphone bawled in
vain. Pungent sweat and heatedly trodden grass, fumes
of tea and porter, thrum of hoofs from the paddock, the
strikings-up and dyings-down of the band all fused into

an extreme for Antonia, whose own senses, boastful, stood up to it.—But then she tripped over a tent peg, jarred the lens in her brain: in the instant, revulsion set in, as it now did always. Like a bullet-hit pane, the whole scene shivered, splintered outward in horror from that small black vacuum in its core. She could not wait to get out—where was Fred? Where was the Ford?

It had come to be six o'clock; midges gauzed the air. Megaphones gave out the raffle results: Maud it was who had won the bottle of whisky and who soon came past bearing her prize. Antonia, having given the child a pound (which, all things considered, she thought enough), snatched the bottle and packed Maud off to find Fred. He arrived, stared, resignedly took Antonia by the elbow and got her through the crowd to the parked car. "Sick?" was all he asked on the drive home. "Only of everything," she replied coldly. Once at Montefort, she uncorked the whisky, he got back into working clothes and was seen no more.

Left behind, Lilia resorted to spending money. The dishevelled stalls by now offered not much choice, but what did remain was being knocked down. She acquired a hand-painted crock of bath salts, some particles of coconut fudge, a nosegay of woollen flowers to pin on, and a Lalique-like amber glass salad bowl. Having given up hoping to know where Jane was, she then set off to track down Maud, to ask *her* how they ever were to get home. But the child, found at the clock golf, merely reiterated loudly: "Cousin Antonia owes me much more money!"

"Or does your father intend us to stay all night?"

"I don't know.—What have you got in that bag?"

"Nothing for you."

"Oh, sweets."

"Oh, don't argue, Maud! And do come: it's time we were going."

Maud, for some reason, respected this academic statement: she gave a finishing lick to her ice-cream cone, stacked up her punnets of oozing strawberries, and preceded her mother to the car park, where they stood about in the dust watching others go. "If you ever knew anyone," Maud remarked, "we'd have got offered a ride home." Lilia expected to faint, so it came at last to their placing themselves under compliment to a stranger, who detoured to drop them at the Montefort gates. "No idea there was anyone living here," he confessed, with a glance of renewed amazement at Lilia's hat. Maud undid the chain, Lilia gave a reproving bow: mother and child set off down the extinct avenue. And there, of course, in front of the house was Fred in the act of starting the Ford to fetch them! Lilia swept indoors past him without a word, hid the fudge inside the hall clock, and went on into the drawingroom.

Inside the drawingroom, facing the door, a mirror

embosked in gilt ferns filled up an alcove. Lilia therefore advanced to meet a figure fit for the Royal Garden
Party—white cartwheel hat, gloves to the elbow, crêpe
floral gown. She and her image confronted each other
and the day's disillusionment, of which the marvel was
that it should recur—summer after summer, the same
story. Who else was to know what *had* been hoped for,
always, in spite of all? Disappointment forever is fresh
and young—she could no longer sustain it; she turned
away and, vanishing from her own eyes, started frowning and fretting over a tea-stain on a fingertip of one of
her white silk gloves. Damage: that was what it all came
down to!

Air had died in here, the windows having been bolted
before they started for the Fête; nor indeed was the
drawingroom often resorted to. Lilia had failed with it
—cretonne tacked to the window-seats, one or two
ruched taffeta cushions, and a magazine-rack only, today, survived from her few attempts to bring the room
into line with her ideas. As against that, she had wreaked
a negative vengeance on what she found here, on anything which might have been here before. Any charm
of a chattery circle had been broken by condemnatory
pushing apart and back of armchairs, "occasional"
chairs, and sofas; exposed to fade still more, an expanse
of carpet remained for Kathie to sweep when she had
time; and the effect, according to mood, was either that

there had lately been a catastrophe or that there was about to be a performance. Ornaments—ruby Bohemian goblets, Dresden cupids, cameos, shells, pagodas, fruit-painted china, filigree silver ware—detected in a conspiracy to collect dust, had been banished to cabinets behind whose misted glaze they each year more dolefully disappeared. Watercolours, whose justification was that they covered stains on the walls, here or there dotted the damask paper; and pelmets, again with gilded ferns, topped off the windows' undraped stare. Uneasily light by day, at night slow to darken, the room seemed to be waiting, perhaps forever, for its dismantlement to be complete. Shreds of butterflies clung to the cornice, out of reach of the mop.

Yet the tide might turn. To the marble chimneypiece Jane, on one of her visits, had restored a pair of fluted pink cornucopias, into which she sometimes remembered to stick roses; and some other hand had propped up, between the two, a large and lovely unframed photograph—one of Antonia's studies of Jane in childhood. Lilia, eying another space, pictured her amber salad bowl here also, wondered where it had got to, but lost heart. Under a window was a scroll-ended sofa: she took off her hat, lay down, disposed the folds of her dress, and began a headache. After some time Fred opened the door from the diningroom and said dubiously: "We were thinking of having supper."

"Do as you please," said she.

"What about you?"

"Today you surpassed yourself."

"Oh?—Sorry."

"Abandoning us. I did not know where to look."

He blinked and said: "Antonia just wants cheese. Where does Kathie keep it?"

"You may well ask."

"Or isn't there any?—*I* thought I'd been timing things about right."

"Left there in front of everyone, high and dry. Naturally, if I had been *Antonia*—"

"Shut up," he begged, "there's a good girl. Like me to bring you anything—tea?"

"If you wish. Though what I need is an aspirin."

"Or go to bed, why not?"

"Because I would sooner be left in peace."

Seeing that he and she had for years slept at opposite ends of the house, her remark lacked what could have been one point: as notice to him to go, it was so welcome that, out of self-reproach, he stopped there fidgeting in the doorway. "Close in here, isn't it, if you've got a headache?" He advanced, edged his way round the sofa, unbolted the window, and pushed the sash up—outside waited the lovers' evening; in the naïve garden within the fence, stocks were night-scented sweeter, old blue-pink roses lusher, manier, headier than in younger

Junes. Lilia, a hand pressed over her eyes, lay like a
waxen lady with clockwork breathing. "Better now," he
asked hopefully, "or not?"

She gave no sign.

Something caught his eye. "You know your hat's down
here on the floor?"

"Yes. Why?"

"That hat of yours—wasn't it new today?"

"No; same as last year, but for the flower."

"It looked pretty fine on you, I thought."

She rolled her head away and said: "Then don't step
on it."

Fred got himself clear of the danger zone, scratched
one eyebrow, irresolutely looked at her, said: "I'll be
back with the tea, then?"

"Or send Maud."

"Right. Later on, I may go out for a turn—can't lock
up, you see, till the girls get back, which mayn't be for
all hours. All hours," he pictured fondly, "dancing tonight." His protruding dark eyes, showing their whites,
moved; in a trance he stood there all but hearing the
music. "Only pity, pity there's not a moon."

She cried aloud: "Moon—why should they have everything?"

"Oh, come," he said, "you were young once."

"And if I was?—What's that to do with *you?*"

So he left her, as she seemed to him to want to be left,

alone. And so there she still was, awake in the darkness, when—after how long?—Jane, back, came wandering through.

Antonia, on her unwilling way to bed, round about midnight looked into the girl's bedroom. Her nostrils caught a reek of hot wick, as from a candle hastily blown out; but Jane either was sound asleep or chose to seem so—which was the more forbidding. Either way, music was off the air; the day was over; nothing now interposed between Antonia and the grave-lonely night. Slopping a trail of drink from her full tumbler, she pitched away down the passage to her own door. Jane waited only to hear that door shut, was wary a minute longer, then sat up again. She relit her candle, drew out the packet of letters from under her pillow, and went on reading.

THESE letters, all in the same hand, were headed by day-names only—"Tuesday," "Saturday," and so on. They had been removed from their envelopes; nothing showed where they had been written or when posted. The writing-paper varied in kind, and, though not yet so aged as to be discoloured, was soiled at the edges, rubbed at the folds. The rubber band round the packet survived the fall from the trunk only to snap, unre-silient, at the first pull from Jane—how many years does it take for rubber to rot? The ink, sharp in the candlelight, had not faded. She could not fail, however, when first she handled them, to connect these letters with that long-settled dust: her sense of their remoteness from her entitled her to feel they belonged to history. Honour therefore allowed her to make free of them.

To start with, she had hardly even been curious. Sweeping the muslin eagerly downstairs with her, she brought the letters with it chiefly because, in her hurry to quit the attic, she could not stay to put them back in the trunk. Tossing them aside, she had gone on to make much of the rescued dress—measuring it up to herself, shaking fullness back again into the smothered folds, finally hanging it near her window that the stuff might revive in the night air. Yet in the very course of those thoughtless minutes, apprehension within her gathered into a peak: the inner course of her life was about to change, and the cause was somewhere here in the room. She was tired, though only as one is tired after pleasure when one is young, with a sort of exalted languor— lightheaded, drained by an access of intense being, see- ing and feeling, as though she had fasted instead of dancing. Her nerves, tuned up by the hot night, waited, though not in fear. What was to happen? She began to undress, looking around her, partly expectant and partly docile—there *were* the letters, on the top of her desk. She went across and stood weighing them in her hand, distantly wondering—how much had shrivelled to this little? Then the word "obelisk" caught her eye.

Then was it that she gave the tug at the band. When that snapped, down again fell the letters, this time altogether spilled out and showering. Vexed by them, gathering them up, she endeavoured to put them into their former order—for that there *had* been an order, and that it was significant, she did not question—but found that could not be done. This datelessness, because the count of time was being kept in some other way, showed the complicity between two people: but what was Jane to make of it? Only by reading all of them was one to come upon their sequence, the "sooner" or "later" giving them sense and story—and from that undertaking Jane shrank, she thought. She had an optic laziness with regard to "writing" at any time; but there was now more to it—she felt a recoil from, a sensuous distaste or disinclination for, these husks, left to be nothing more by the evaporation from them of passion. At the same time, they inspired reluctant awe, and some misgiving: if there *was* anything in them, let it remain contained!

Jane was without emotional curiosity; her lack of it was neither failure nor chance, but part of a necessary unconcern. She had grown up amid extreme situations and frantic statements; and, out of her feeling for equilibrium, contrived to ignore them as far as possible. Her time, called hers because she was required to live in it and had no other, was in bad odour, and no wonder.

Altogether the world was in a crying state of exaspera-
tion, but that was hardly her fault: too much had been
going on for too long. Like someone bidden to enter an
already overcrowded and overcharged room, she paused
for as long as possible on the threshold, waiting for
something to subside, for the floor to empty or the air to
clear. The passions and politics of her family so much
resembled those of the outside world that she made little
distinction between the two. It was her hope that this
might all die down, from lack of recruits or fuel or, most
of all, if more people were to take less notice. She did
what she could by adding no further heat.

Continuously reflecting, she seldom thought. Apart
from liking having her fortune told, she had no particular attitude to the future, but she had an instinctive
aversion from the past; it seemed to her a sort of pompous imposture; as an idea it bored her; it might not be
too much to say that she disapproved of it. She enjoyed
being: how could it not depress her to realize that the
majority of people no longer were? Most of all she mis-
trusted the past's activity and its queeringness—she knew
no one, apart from her own contemporaries, who did not
speak of it either with falsifying piety or with bitterness;
she sometimes had had the misfortune to live through
hours positively contaminated by its breath. Oh, there
lay the root of evil!—this continuous tedious business
of received grievances, not-to-be-settled old scores. Yes,

so far as she was against anything she was against the past; and she felt entitled to raid, despoil, rifle, balk, or cheat it in any possible way. She gloried in having set free the dress. But the letters—had they not insisted on forcing their own way out?

Jane, in bed, had been deep in the letter holding the word "obelisk" when Antonia's footstep made her blow out the candle. This was the one to which she at once returned, and which, after some few invaded hours of sleep, she had carried outdoors with her next morning, to re-read under the monument itself.

THE family spent that morning mostly apart—except that Jane, at about eleven o'clock, made her way out to the haymaking and her father. No topic therefore was raised until they gathered for midday dinner, which found Antonia in a public mood.

Jane, back again in gingham showing her limbs, slid into her seat at table, all fresh serenity. Fred, pleased with life, came in as far as the doorway still absently towelling his neck; Lilia ladled out stew at arm's length, leaning away to avoid steam, and Maud, having seized the occasion to ask a blessing, now eyed the hotpot, wondering what would come of it. She and Jane faced across at Antonia, who, not wearing sunglasses, had her back to the light. Blinds were down over the open windows, the door through to the passage was propped ajar, and the wallpaper was of a smoky crimson which absorbed some of the glare from outdoors—the diningroom was tolerable enough. The table, no worse for being too large, was spread with a starchless damask cloth, and

two or three pieces of Sheffield plate—biscuit box, mus-
tard pot, trolley for pickle-jars—adorned it for the benefit of Antonia. The dinner plates, patterned with blue
roses, were chipped at the rims; their glaze was fissured
and browned from having often baked too long in the
oven.

Fred slung the towel out through the door to Kathie,
sleeked his hair, unrolled his shirt sleeves, and slumped
into his place at the top of the table; he nodded good
morning to Antonia and began to eat, in his methodical,
rapid, abstracted way. Lilia fanned at herself and the
stew with a paper napkin; Antonia reached for the
water jug; Jane and Maud side-by-side sat silent and
clean. The inappropriateness of the fuming dish to the
torrid day was noted, but only as one more stroke of
fate: Antonia, for one, did not bat an eyelid. Her indifference to all food other than really good made her
slow to distinguish between the bad and the worse—if
she felt queasy she did not appear at all; at other times
she ate enough to pass. On the whole she showed the
best of her character, or at any rate its negative better
side, at meals: seldom in her destructive life had she
criticized what laid itself open, nor could she be bothered taking it out of anyone, particularly Lilia, in the
smaller ways. Her attitude to what was set before her
was therefore gentlemanly or rational—had one hoped
to eat well, one should not have put Lilia here. She

now, having drunk water, put down her glass and took up her fork. "And how are we all, after all that?" she genially asked, looking round the table. "You, for instance," turning to him, "Fred?"

He blinked at having been singled out, swallowed, and asked her: "After all what?"

"Our gaiety."

"What, yesterday?" He was forced to empty his mouth. "By the look of it, they should have taken in money—record, I should wonder."

"Any idea how much?"

"Four hundred and ninety-eight pounds, sixteen and five pence," Maud volunteered.

"Who asked *you?*" asked her mother. "And gross or net?"

"Time will show," said the child, looking down her nose.

Antonia mused: "The country's rotten with money, if one could touch it. Why not a fête to promote us, here?"

Lilia, in a discouraging tone, said: "And what would they all do here?—all jump off the rock?"

"So," Antonia went on, this time to Jane, "you ended by haymaking?"

"Yes I did.—What about my pay?" the girl demanded radiantly of her father, who replied: "Not for less than a day's work."

"She works in her way," said Antonia. "She's always

company, Fred.—Naturally she'll have told you about
her letter?"

"Had you a letter?" he asked Jane.

"Dear Fred, it's been the talk of the morning!"

"Antonia, don't be hateful," said Jane calmly.

"There happened to *be* nothing for Jane this morning," Lilia still more crushingly interposed. "I know, as
I took in the post myself—what was for you, Antonia, I
sent up."

"Yes, thank you: bills, as no doubt you saw.—No,
Jane's didn't come by the postman; nothing so boring.
She helped herself to it, out of a trunk—we are inclined
to think it was not to her."

"Of course it was not: how could it be? I told you,"
Jane said, beginning to colour up. "It, they, fell out
when I took the dress."

"You're far too quick to assume that people are dead."

"The trunk was up in the attics," Jane told her father,
as though in justice to him if not to herself she ought to
give the entire picture, in the as nearly as possible
proper light. "And there a hat was up there, rather like
Lady Latterly's. (I must go back for that; I forgot it!)"

"Those musty attics," Lilia remarked. "Everything up
there belongs to Antonia." She yawned and piercingly
rang a handbell for Kathie to bring in pudding and
change the plates. Jane sat like a statue till this was done,
then said: "But so does everything in this house."

"Somehow, Jane," said Antonia, "that sounds un-
friendly."

"I don't see why."

"To start with, I've no idea what *is* in the house.
Never have I known, and I never want to—by this time,
who could know, and however should they? Not I, certainly: God forbid! Yet I can't help wondering what
you've unburied—there may be much (I should think
there probably is) that we should all do far better to
leave alone."

Lilia, who seldom addressed her elder daughter,
turned her head aside to avoid any air of doing so, while
she nonetheless felt called upon to explain: "What Antonia means, and she has the right to do so, is, why were
you interfering with her things?"

"Almost that," half-agreed Antonia smoothly, "though
not altogether, perhaps, quite." Her eyes and Jane's met
across the table. Up to now Jane's acting of the chidden
and disconcerted favourite had been no more than in
the convention, but now there *was* a tremor—resistance,
query, reproach, but above all a sort of disassociation
showed in her unswerving long blue gaze. Not she but
Antonia had gone too far this time. The moment declared itself, and sharply—Antonia brought out her
cigarettes and with nervous egocentricity lit up. (She
seldom, at Montefort, smoked till a meal was done.)

Antonia's eyes were darker than Jane's in colour, and
more human. Their surrounds had a smoky, smudged
look which was picturesque, and endemic: she did not
use mascara—these were Irish eyes, communicative and
often hostile, sunk in a face which had, more or less, by
now come to look cosmopolitan. Cheek bones wore
rouge like an ingrained tarnish; the hair, from which
the effects of expert cutting, tinting, and burnishing
were at Montefort beginning to wear off, was raked upward, exposing the hardy forehead. The mouth would
have been forcible without paint, the jaw had kept its
angular outline, and the skin wore well in spite of all—
it, too, had the benefit of sporadic care. She had kept up
her looks, such as they were, while showing a slapdash
disregard for them. Antonia's face, in spite of its show
of indolence, had something energetic about the cast of
it—nothing sagged except when she foresaw death; there
were hollows, tensions, and shadows, but they were
speaking ones, kept in play by the contrarieties of her
mood, the many dissonances of her nature. What was in
her stayed unresigned, untaught; when she scowled, a
mutinous heaviness clouded down on her. It was a dan-
ger-signal (now to be read) when she chose to imitate
impassivity.

She today wore an orange canvas Mediterranean shirt,
closely knotted up at the neck with a string of false

pearls. Rolled-up sleeves bared her strong forearms, which slendered down when it came to the wrists and hands.

Reflecting, she stubbed out the cigarette. "What a fuss we make! But so little happens."

Fred, with a touch of contempt, said: "What's happening now?"

"One would like to know."

His comment was to grasp the pitcher of custard and measure out dollops on to his plate of fruit. As Jane pushed the sugar bowl his way, he teasingly, with confidence, spent a glance on her: "What have *you* been up to that I don't know of?" He no more cared than knew: she was in his sight, she had been his own all the later, greater part of this morning. She removed the pitcher from between them, letting it round again to the receptive Maud, then smiled back: "Nothing that *you'd* call anything."

"Good enough, then," he said to his spoon and fork.

"Falling in love with a love letter," said Antonia.

Maud, even, found this worthy of note; she turned to examine her sister's profile. Lilia ingested the statement slowly, thought, then began to express surprise. "To me it's rather peculiar that in spite of her chances, all we hear about London, and that keeping on dancing yesterday night, Jane should have to stoop for romance to a musty trunk belonging to who knows who? Myself, I should have been sorry to, but times alter. *Are* there no men about who are good enough?—*Maud,* I thought I said no more custard!"

"No, you forgot to."

"And after *how* many eggs, with your blood upset?"

"Oh, don't nag her; dose her, for heaven's sake!" burst out Fred, with a sudden twitch of the forehead. Maud, not in need of a partisan, drew herself away and became remote; the women at table stared. There ensued an astounded pause, in the course of which he flicked a glance at his wrist-watch; as for Jane, she might never have been there. He thrust his chair back and stood up: "If you'll all excuse me, got to be off."

"Why, what's the rush?" inquired Antonia, while Lilia languidly pointed out: "You won't be getting the men back under their hour."

"Want to look at the tractor."

"Heavens, trouble again?"

"It seemed to be going all right this morning," Jane said in a low and concerned tone, "at least, *I* thought so."

He flatly told her: "This morning isn't this afternoon."

"How true that is," said Antonia, "and how often sad." Lilia, lolling her eyes down at her folded arms, remarked from a distance: "*I* cannot help whatever it is that has now upset you."

" 'Upset'?" he cried, knocking the word away. "But if you'd like to know why I've had enough, it's this everlasting maunder about those attics.—You, Antonia, it must be twenty times I've asked you to get that stuff at the top cleared out—burned, junked, sold, shifted: I don't care what. I've offered you the pack of men for the job. I *need* that space, I tell you! I'm short of storage."

"What would you put up there—oats?"

"I won't have those dragged upstairs," put in Lilia firmly, "bringing in rats."

Fred rolled his eyes. "Whoever said I said oats?"

"Antonia did."

"Well, listen to what I'm saying!"

"Why should I, when you're seldom addressing me?" Lilia paused, told Maud she might now be excused from table (the child, however, chose to stay where she was), then added: "Although I must say, Fred, your objection to those attics is very sudden: it's been my nerves they've been always upon—everything not only dirty but so inflammable day and night up there over our heads, with Kathie and who knows who going through with candles."

Maud stated: "Kathie is too scared."

"It's not especially Kathie I'm referring to—though I've heard *you* prancing up there, from time to time, Maud, with your hobgoblin."

"No, I am the one," Jane easily said. "But if I'd started a fire, you'd know by now."

"We think we do," said Antonia. "That's what's the matter. We think we can smell burning; or at any rate the beginning of burning, smouldering. What have you done? You have an igniting touch—wouldn't you, now, say so?" she threw at Fred. Not yet gone, unable to go, he stood leaning heavily on his hands, which gripped and shifted along the chair-back, tilting the chair up. Jane, at the instant, turned to her father also, with an air of waiting upon his verdict. He frowned; his eyes were not to be met; he told her: "Tell 'em to go to blazes," which sounded less like advice than a sort of plea.

Antonia smiled: "Oh, Jane would never do that."

"Yes, I would. Do go to blazes, Antonia."

"But tell us—who are your letters from?"

" 'From'?" echoed Lilia, then had to think again: this was hard to formulate. "How can they be 'from' when they're not *to* her?"

"Still, come on, Jane. Otherwise one might guess."

Jane, by one of her miracles, had recovered nerve, effrontery, or whatever the moment took. She first put down her spoonful of gooseberries, as a sort of concession to their anxiety, then drew her fingers slowly across her forehead, as it were as a dragnet for her thoughts.

That having failed, she regretfully shook her head, till all at once she grew bright with the perfect answer. "They are simply signed with a squirl."

Antonia, stone-still while Jane deliberated, jumped as though something had struck the table: ostentatiously, however, she still said nothing, merely nodding across at Jane once or twice. In what had become an all-round hush Maud said grace loudly, then left the diningroom —in the stone passage outside she was to be heard scuffling and sparring with her familiar, Gay David, wrongly referred to by Lilia as a hobgoblin, who was not admitted by her to family meals. Smells of old oil from the incubator outside the kitchen for the first time travelled in through the open door: all the senses were sharpened. Fred raised his eyebrows, whistled a silent bar, let go the chair-back and followed Maud out. He was to be felt gone. Lilia it was who now, in a stony voice, declared: "In that case, those letters are mine."

"Whatever makes you think that?"

"The way you go on, Antonia. *And* what Jane said."

"Poor Jane's said practically nothing."

Lilia said: "It's been more than enough."

"I only do wish," said the girl, "that I had said absolutely nothing. Then there need never have been this. From now on I shall; I mean I shall not. But of course it's been you, Antonia, who have done the talking; because you, I imagine, know more than I do, or may

think you care very much more. I feel rather foolish—
do you mind if I go?" She deferentially sat, awaiting the
word from one or another of the transfixed women. Not
a sign having come, she seemed forced to add: "So, I
suppose it *is* Cousin Guy? I wondered, but I'd never
have thought one could tie up a 'G' into such a knot."

"It could be done," said Antonia, "and it was."

"The rest of the writing's not really difficult, once you
come to know it."

"How *dared* you, poking and prying?" cried out Lilia.

Antonia, at nervous work with her thumb-nail dis-
lodging a gooseberry seed from her lower teeth, broke
off to say: "Lilia, I shouldn't brood."

"And why should I not?"

"I could hardly tell you.—Who *are* they to?" Antonia
asked off-hand, still giving attention to the seed.

"They have no beginnings," Jane answered, weighing
the question calmly. "I mean to say, they simply begin.
So I cannot help. And I shall not show them; I cannot
see why I should."

"Why indeed?" asked Antonia, so agreeably as to
make this all go flat. She could not even be bothered to
speak again till she had finished tightening her pearl
slip-knot and twisting her neck to see if she had choked
herself. "Naturally, finding's keeping," she then announced. Lilia's failure to see things in that light was
marked by a complete absence of all expression—reach-

ing round her, she began to stack plates on plates, dishes on dishes. But sweat broke out on her forehead and upper lip: it was afternoon, most brutal phase of the day, which had leapt upon and was demolishing the poor snow-woman. She forgot the plates and began to pluck at the deep V-neck of her cotton dress, desperately trying to fan air down it; until the humidity starting up even in the insides of her elbows made her unjoint and drop her arms like a doll's. She leaned back in her chair to gasp, and her back adhered like a stamp to the curved mahogany. Lilia's being so humblingly overcome worked upon the others as nothing else could—Antonia writhed inside her own body; Jane turned away to contemplate a darkened oil-painting of hilly forests.

Lilia said: "I'm in no state to argue."

"Then don't worry."

"But it seems to me, private letters are private letters."

"That's how it apparently seems to Jane."

The girl remarked: "There's a stag in that picture I never saw."

"They never, never were *to* her," Lilia averred, in a voice of not yet exhausted scorn.

Antonia shrugged. "She likes to feel that they are."

That brought Jane back slowly from the painting, with something of its phantasmagoric and distant oddness still in her eyes. "Thank you for explaining for me," she said, without irony though also without the ironic love for Antonia she had seldom not shown. "You so nearly understand so well." In the act of getting up from her chair, she hesitated for a chivalrous moment towards Lilia, but after all could think of nothing to say, or at least of nothing not better left unsaid. So she quitted them, taking her plate and her father's away with her and into the kitchen, where Kathie was sitting over her dinner.

Out through the kitchen back door, into the yard. The slate roofs sent shimmers up; the red doors ajar all seemed caught by a spell in the act of opening; white outbuildings tottered there in the glare. Grass which had seeded between the cobbles, parched and dying, deadened her steps: a visible silence filled the place— long it was since anyone had been here. Slime had greenly caked in the empty trough, and the unprecedented loneliness of the afternoon looked out, as through eyelets cut in a mask, from the archways of the forsaken dovecote. Not a straw stirred, or was there to stir, in the kennel; and above her something other than clouds was missing from the uninhabited sky. Nothing was to be known. One was on the verge, however, possibly, of more.

Jane, going into the walled garden, made her way round the end of the house under the sightless Venetian window: she roamed zigzag across the garden, and, getting out again through a gap, found herself facing the

sealike uplands. Step quickening, she kept in close to
the flank of the woods raggedly edging the river gorge.
Some way along, an elder grew leaning forward, its
branches clotted with waxen blossom within themselves
forming a cave. Heavy was the scent, rank the inside
darkness which filtered through. The girl, having
reached the spot, without hesitation parted the branches
and dived between them.

For the women left behind in the diningroom, it became impossible to remain together, alone with the
situation, once Jane had gone. If they eyed one another,
it had been only in wonder as to which of them could
get out of the room first. Lilia had acted—ringing the
bell for Kathie, then giving out that, herself, she must lie
down. She had been heard ascending the stairs as though
to some further degree of martyrdom. Antonia, some
minutes later, moved across to a window, pulled up the
blind, put on her sunglasses, and, seating herself aslant
on the sill, stared out diagonally across the country. She
did not know what she expected, until she caught the
far-away pink flicker of Jane's frock disappearing into
the flowering elder. "So that's where she has hidden
them," she then knew.

§ IV

ANTONIA thought: "So there *is* more to happen."

Life works to dispossess the dead, to dislodge and oust them. Their places fill themselves up; later people come in; all the room is wanted. Feeling alters its course, is drawn elsewhere, or seeks renewal from other sources. When of love there is not enough to go round, inevitably it is the dead who must go without: we tell ourselves that they do not depend on us, or that they have not our requirements. Their continuous dying while we live, their repeated deaths as each of us dies who knew them, are not in nature to be withstood. Obstinate rememberers of the dead seem to queer themselves or show some signs of a malady; in part they come to share the dead's isolation, which it is not in their power to break down—for the rest of us, so necessary is it to let the dead go that we expect they may be glad to be gone. Greatest of our denials to them is a part to play: it appears that they now cannot touch or alter whatever may be the existent scene—not only are they not here to participate,

65

but there would be disorder if they *were* here. Their being left behind in their own time caused estrangement between them and us, who must live in ours.

But the recognition of death may remain uncertain, and while that is so, nothing is signed and sealed. Our sense of finality is less hard-and-fast: two wars have raised their query to it. Something has challenged the law of nature: it is hard, for instance, to see a young death in battle as in any way the fruition of a destiny, hard not to sense the continuation of the apparently cut-off life, hard not to ask, but *was* dissolution possible so abruptly, unmeaningly, and soon? And if not dissolution, instead, what? This had been so, so far, for Antonia in the case of her cousin Guy: yes, though a generation was mown down, his death seemed to her an invented story. Not that it was unlike him to be killed—lightly he had on the whole taken that for granted; they all sooner or later were: why should he not be?—but that it was unlike him to be dead. She knew he had not envisaged that, not entertained the idea of it for a moment. His sense of connection, of consequence, had been always faulty: death, yes, why not?—but deadness, no. What was a man like Guy ever to make of *that?* He and life had had much the same tricky temperament; they kept one another in play; they were on terms. It would be long before Guy was done with life. . . . Antonia's reading of the War Office telegram had been followed by a blasphemous incredulity which she could not believe to be hers alone.

What in her had outwardly passed for grief had seemed to her to be something of his frenzy. She recollected how he had kicked a door down when a defective lock kept him stuck in a lavatory during a tennis party —he was a participator: how could he be expected to cease to act or agree to hold off? She could have felt something irreligious about an attempt to see Guy's quandary in a religious light. He had had it in him to make a good end, but not soon; he would have been ready to disengage himself when the hour came, but rightfully speaking it had not. Earthbound?—no, she was never to think of him like that, nor had he the makings of any ghost. It was simply that these years she went on living belonged to him, his lease upon them not having run out yet. The living were living in his lifetime; and of this his contemporaries—herself, Lilia, Fred—never were unaware. They were incomplete.

So it had gone on. Meantime, another war had peopled the world with another generation of the not-dead, overlapping and crowding the living's senses still more with the senses left by unlived lives. Antonia and others younger were creatures of an impossible time, breathing in wronged air—air either too empty or too full, one could not say which. Jane, on the other hand, unaware of loss, should be taken to be in balance perfectly: she had come late enough (had she not?) to be at no known disadvantage. What *she* thought, no one had thought of asking until this morning—but then, what an alien she'd seemed to be!

Somewhere away in the fields the tractor jerked back again into sound.

From the woods the elder stood out, like a chalked mark. What a stupid hiding-place, what a cramped bower—just room to sit on one's heels inside! Nettles there would be, an old tin lid left behind after some rite of Maud's—that thicket held, though Jane might not know it, signs of its infestation by many childhoods. Or was the elder masking a secret gateway, outlet of a precipitous brambled dog-path to the river? Had the girl gone down breakneck to where, near Gay David's Hole, light from the current ran up the rock? Antonia pictured all but the act of reading.

Kathie wandered in to clear the diningroom table; she stopped behind Antonia's shoulder to join her in staring out of the window. "Nothing much to see," she ventured to say.

"I suppose not."

"Miss, the wasps are beginning."

"Tell them I've gone to the sea," commanded Antonia, with a sudden, inspired pluck at her pearls.

"Tell the wasps, is it?"

"No, the mistress when she comes down."

Kathie, off to the table with her tray, asked: "Is it true you're going? They say the sea's as far as you can go."

"That's why."

"And there's no end to it, once you'd get there.—And Miss Jane also?"

"No.—And cut me a sandwich."

"Out of what?—She'll be lonely after you."

"No.—Out of whatever you have."

"There's the shop ham.—Am I to say to Miss Jane you're gone to the sea?"

"As you like; but cut me the sandwich now. And first, for heaven's sake wash your hands!"

Kathie glanced down at her hands with some curiosity. "Miss," she asked, "do you mean to go *on* the sea?"

"In it."

"Then that would be swimming.—You'd never drown?"

"I never could," said Antonia regretfully.

"Only wait, then," Kathie exclaimed, "till we find the sandwich!"

Five minutes later Antonia filled her flask, pitched what more she needed into the back of the Ford, and drove away: it would be about forty miles. The Ford tearing off down the avenue was heard by Lilia, who went to her bedroom window to try to see who was in it, but too late. There being at least one person gone from the place somehow lessened the pressure on Montefort;

yet as against that, one felt more deserted. Nobody had spoken of any plans. In her kimono she sighed and returned to bed, to a pillow clammy though not with tears. Meantime, the outgoing Ford's sound not only fanned out widely over the country but entered the valley, where the low-running river slipped on its way between necks of sand and archipelagos of little dry stones. The summer-idle water dawdled in shallows, slid on in skeins where it had brightly appeared to be least moving, and in a tea-brown clear pool mirrored the cliff above. Also Maud was photographed on the water, crouched on the ledge of Gay David's Hole, a small low cave under the cliff's face. *"Ca-ar!"* she bawled across to Jane.

Jane lay face down among growing bracken, on the Montefort side. Water-mint wet in the dwindling current and meadowsweet creamily frothing the river bank sent up a scented oblivion round her; a hot tang came from the bracken fronds crushed into bedding by her body. Languidly she neither answered nor raised her head, merely caught at a frond by the tip, bending it down to let a ladybird make its way more easily. "Car, car, car!" Maud repeated, each time for emphasis punching Gay David in the unseen ribs. The ladybird paused as though it could hear; Jane yawned, pushed her hands up into her hair, and, for peace's sake, shouted back: "Not the tractor?"

"No: our car: too fast." Maud again fiercely harkened. "It's gone now."

"Yes."

"Suppose Satan's got it?"

"Suppose He has." This time indifference caused Jane's voice to fade out halfway across the river. *"Wha-at?"* insisted the child.

"Nothing—nothing—nothing." On that descending note Jane again became as she was before, letting the deep keen dream come combing through her, keeping her being running like tressy water-weed, like Ophelia's drowned hair. Nowhere was silence: flies droned over the bracken, far off the tractor patiently drew the mower —and at the instant, with a cave-echoed splash Maud swung her legs into the pool; while all through the minutes conspiratorially the child and her familiar gabbled together in the afternoon distance across the river. Yet all blent into a sort of hush.

The particular secret of the place where Jane lay was that it was pre-inhabited. An ardent hour of summer had gone by here—yes, *here,* literally where she was, to her certain knowledge. Evidence was in the breast of her dress, the letter. This narrow tract of the valley had been thought in, as a walker waded through the resilient bracken or stood, looking up at the cliff, here where the turf itself broke off into a miniature cliff this side of the

water. It had been June then too: everything he had
said he saw stamped the scene again, so that the landscape became a vision and Jane could hardly believe it
was still before her. But it was, and not only still here
but poetically immortal; and, better still, it had comi-
calities which his eye had noted—out of the cliff, for
instance, out of the vagaries and traceries of the limestone *did* look a clown's face, ferns for eyebrows, loony
eye-hollows, neb awry, fallen-open mouth where the
cave yawned; and the clown did seem to be swallowing
terrified gold fish as light-spangles went darting under
the rock. And here, three paces from where she lay, was
the thorn tree; also part of the story, for that it grew
wickedly crooked he had perceived, passing for a minute
into its shadow then out again into the golden-yellow
beyond. But all this he had been beholding not for its
own sake only; through it he was seeking a speaking lan-
guage—he was in love. *"I thought,"* he wrote *"if only
you had been here!"*

A thread lay dropped on the grass, for Jane to pick up.
"But here *I* am. Oh, here I *am!"* she protested.

Seeing how brief all time was, it seemed impossible
she could be too late: this valley held waiting in its keeping, suspense in the glitter of its air. Here was the hour,
still to be lived! Impatient, the letter shifted inside her
dress as, rolling over, she put an ear to the ground, to
one of the turfy spaces between bracken, to seem to be

hearing returning footsteps as a pulse in her head started to beat down. Between him and her dwindled the years: where indeed was he if not beside her? They could not now miss one another, surely?

His letter had been no more than delayed on its way to her.

Footsteps, however, came no nearer. To bring herself into unmistakable view Jane got up and, dazzled, stood thigh-deep in the bracken, shading her eyes—to be *seen,* there was no one this side of the river. Almost in actual despair she walked to the thorn tree, the wicked witness, propitiatingly to rub its bark with her hand.

"What are *you* playing?" yelled out the observant Maud.

"Nothing," Jane cried back—dismayed, affronted.

"*Oh,* no you're not!"

Jane searched the cliff: its face of the clown was gone—below it the water, disenchanted, now wore nothing but Maud's reflection. And even while one looked, the child moved from her station over the pool, edging her way on the narrowing rock-lip till, that ended, she swung on tufts of ivy. Her sister, instinctively fending off, cried: "Oh, Maud, why can't you stay where you were?"

"Because it's tea-time." Maud, frock stuffed into her drawers, already answered from mid-stream, picking her way onward from shoal to shallow.

"What is?" Jane asked, backing against the thorn tree. "Now is."

"Then don't tell them I'm here."

"Who cares? Cousin Antonia's out—unless that *was* Satan." Maud, having made the landing, tore off fistfuls of bracken to scratch her legs with. "Nothing cools my blood today, even water," she stated, suffering on the bank; then, with one of her closer looks: "What are you pretending about that tree?"

"This tree?" Jane guiltily dropped her hand.

"Just wondered what *you* were making up," explained the child, with the air of a connoisseur.

"Nothing."

Maud raised her eyebrows, causing Jane to go on: "I don't spy on you; why should you spy on me?"

"Why pick on *my* place, then, to be so peculiar in, when there are miles of places where no one else is? I didn't bother to watch you, I simply saw you. But you performed as though you meant to be watched. However."

" 'However' is Mother's word."

Maud merely said: "What else am I not to tell?"

"Do go and have your disgusting tea."

Maud made her sedate way up to the house by the track used by the water-cart; not for her were dog-paths, down one of which Jane had made her ecstatic descent. Instinct had not lied: tea was on the table. The early

wasp was already probing at last year's jam, fatalistically
watched by Lilia, who sat there over her lonely cup. "No
cake?" Maud asked, looking round as she sat down.

Her mother replied: "Cousin Antonia's gone to the
sea."

Maud confined herself to eating and drinking.

"Anyone else would have taken a child like you; as it
is, she's even forgotten Jane.—Where's Jane?"

"She doesn't want any tea."

"I hardly wonder," said Lilia, "all things considered."

"*Is* it five o'clock?"

"How am I to know?"

The designing glance darted by Maud at the radio in
the corner caused Lilia with passion to declare: "And I
won't have you running after Big Ben!" Maud shrugged
her shoulders inside her narrow frock; her mother put
down her cup, adding: "I'm beginning to think I'm ill
with all the monomania in this house."

She spoke as one in search of a fellow-being; her conviction that she was gripped by something mortal made
it frightening to be left alone with a child. Her inner
face, by now gaunt with solitude, looked out not without nobility through the big white mask padded with
flesh. Sorrow was there in front of her like an appari-
tion: she saw now, with belated dread, what life had
proved to be, what it had made of her. Could there have

been an otherwise, an alternative? Who was to tell her, who was to know? She did not pity herself, for there is an austere point at which even self-pity halts, forbidden. Loss had been utter; not till today had she wholly taken account. Guy was dead, and only today at dinner had she sorrowed for him.

What had now happened must either kill her or, still worse, force her to live: automatically she pressed her hand under her breast on the heart side, testing her lungs at the same time with an uncertain deep breath. "Who here," she went on to ask, "ever thinks of others? I daresay I myself could have been a more loving mother to you and Jane, but, as things are, neither of you require me. I should hardly call us a family. I admit your father works hard to keep us, but sometimes I imagine he wonders why."

Maud said: "I suppose, because we were born."

"You know, Maud, I had little to say to that. You never would have been here had things turned out differently; and as it is, your father had small reward."

"Halving everything up with Cousin Antonia?" Maud said, taking a spoon to the melting butter.

"I don't consider Jane even halved. Seldom does she permit him to speak to Jane; that is, when the girl *is* allowed home. Now we see what comes of it—making a game of everything!"

"Cousin Antonia loses her temper at games."

"You're too old for your age, Maud."

"Well, look at today."

"Leave today alone."

"Banging off down the avenue in our motor—"

"I said, that's enough!"

The child, turning to stare, said: "Are you missing Cousin Antonia?"

That was it: Maud had hit the nail on the head. Who, today, *but* Antonia was the fellow-being? Everything had the two women gone through together; not least, the being against each other. At dinner that outrage had struck at them both, and, while they tried to turn it against each other, had made them one—thirty years, yes, and more, had led up to this. Animosity itself had become a bond, whose deep-down tightening suddenly made itself felt today. Antonia's half of the past fitted in to Lilia's: looking back, one saw through both lives the progress of the unfinished story. Thrown together, they had adhered: virtually, nothing more than this had happened to them since their two girlhoods. Thanklessly, intimacy had insisted on being theirs: how, indeed, could either have lived without it? Through bickerings, jibings, needlings, recriminations, sulks, traps set, points scored, ignominies inflicted, they had remained in communication; their warfare met their unwilling need for contact with, awareness of, one another. Almost no experience, other than Guy and their own dissonance,

could they be said to have had in common; and yet it
was what they *had* had in common which riveted them.
For worse or better, they were in each other's hands.
Such a relationship is lifelong.

Today, at this very table, had they not both trembled,
both feeling the same hand once more upon the door?

Conquering, violating Jane—born of Lilia cold, by
Antonia rendered colder—what had she done or been
caused to do? Ready, empty, apt—the inheritor; foreign
in her beauty with the foreignness of this supplanting
new time. Jane, so removed by school education, taking
out her trial lesson in love! Not so much the unlikeness
of Jane to herself now, but the non-correspondence between Jane's youth and her own had drained any hope
of kinship from Lilia's motherhood. This idol of Fred's,
this golden changeling was, in so far as she belonged to
anybody, Antonia's—but see, today, how even Antonia
had been out-monstered.

"Wherever *is* Jane? Whatever is she up to?" Lilia restlessly asked Maud.

The child returned: "How old would be Cousin
Guy?"

"When?"

"Now. Getting on, like you all?"

"I never speak of him, as you know, Maud."

The child sat rather queerly biting her thumb, till
Lilia uneasily said: "Well, what?"

"I wonder how long anyone lasts."

At the instant, almost without a sound, Lady Latterly's chauffeur-driven Daimler slid into view and drew up outside the windows. The man sat in profile for long enough to recover from what seemed to be a surprise, then respectfully got out: he placed his gauntlet upon the gate of the little fence. Lilia, appalled, slowly put her hands to her hair; Maud dived under the table, emerged on all fours, in this manner travelled the carpet, and, at eye-level with the window-sill, made a swift reconnaissance. A corgi out for the drive and sumptuous daylight, only, occupied the back of the car; the chauffeur, now at the front door, was still failing to find either bell or knocker.

"Come with a note," Maud said. "It could have come on a bicycle." She was off in a flash, however, to the front door, coming back again a degree more slowly to announce to Lilia: "It's addressed to Jane."

"It's for her, then. Put it down on the table."

"They want an answer."

"I can't help that, when she's out."

"He says her ladyship says to wait."

The idea of that agitated Lilia beyond proportion: the truth was she had a neurosis about anyone standing outside a door—it linked with the sense she'd had since she came to Montefort of being besieged, under observation, or in some way even under a threat. Apprehension was seldom at rest in her, nor indeed were there enough comers to Montefort to wear down fear by familiarity— no calls to the telephone for there was not a telephone, no vans delivering, seldom a passer-by, no neighbours to speak of; even the postman, during Antonia's absences, for days together gave them a wide berth. When in winter, sometimes, the hunt ran over the land and Maud and Kathie ran whooping out, she trembling locked herself into her bedroom. Was it the place itself, her mistrust of Ireland, or the uncanny attentiveness of the country which kept her nerves ever upon the stretch? What was unforeseen boded something abnormal. So, as some dread the telegraph boy, she dreaded any comer at all—men wanting Fred, tinkers with their sky-empty blue eyes annihilating their patter of talk, beggar-women sepulchral in black shawls, with the saints behind them. Worst were those who stood at the door mute, neither speaking nor going away.

But today everything must be faced—Lilia, tightening round the mouth, pushed past Maud to take a look herself. Obliquely, round the bobbled edge of the curtain, she sized up the commissar-like figure of the chauffeur. "Giving us orders," she said to Maud. "I suppose you're expected to find Jane?"

"I could, if I liked."

"Well, you better had. We can't have *him* there."

The chauffeur, overhearing or not, reclasped Martian gauntlets behind his back: he was staring in the other direction, faceless. That uniform of his was disaster-dark among the feckless front-garden roses. Maud, about to make off into the wilds with the note, squinted once more at the written-on blue envelope, remarking: "This time a letter is really *to* her." Lilia, rather than hear more, dived her top part out of the open window: she coughed till the chauffeur turned gravely round. "Go back and sit in the car," she over-loudly said to him, "why don't you?"

He sprang to the peak of his cap, with a "Thank you, madam," and she, surprised at his having a face at all, on the instant thought: "What waste of a man!" Weakly elated after the broken nightmare, she tottered back to her place at the tea table to pour herself out yet another cup, to stare fixedly while the man obeyed her: the fence gate twanged, the car door shut. He was again in profile, within watch by her eye should she care to watch. Though with time the Daimler seemed to begin to subside from view, as though there were quicksands in front of Montefort.

It took the whole of Maud's cunning to find Jane. Revulsion had driven the elder sister out from the valley, shame drove her far from the river or very thought of it. Humiliation caused her to pluck Guy's letter like an asp from her breast: blindly she scrambled uphill with it to entomb it under the flat stone under the stifling elder. There its fellows were. The naïvety, as she saw it now, of the hiding-place made a farce of the letters, the love, herself. Who cared if anyone *were* to find them? Having stamped the stone down, she turned away, that caricatured hour beside the river ever remorselessly before her eyes. Not having been seen by Maud, but what Maud *saw:* that was what so appalled her! She was made a fool of. And shown up: yes, as the thing she was, without norm or nature—she, who having humanity waiting round her everywhere in this pathetic house, would have none of it: it was not good enough for her. Oh, how the vice of uncaringness had been hers; she had neither heart nor wish for a living creature—smiling, she humoured, temporized, so got by. Scalded by unredeeming tears, she fought through the undergrowth round the elder, twigs scornfully whipping at her face. What *was* this that grew like a danger in her? What had she been tempted up to the very brink of? Was she lost forever? Was there a path back?

To and fro she wandered, body and mind: outraged. Thrusting feelings rose to a panic in her—in extremity she was her mother's daughter, baffled, unable to word thoughts. Her sunny outward "finish," work of Antonia, had been but a certain giving of grace to the girl's not having of what she had not—behind all lay a misgiving, an ineptitude. Now she tried to think, as a form of moral endeavour, but had to perceive that she never could, or, if she desired to be herself, never must. Everybody (this was enough to realize) was fathomlessly angry with her, and no wonder. What she felt was, she had better get back to London—at once, tomorrow if not today. She pictured streets, and herself anonymous. Why not bolt now, before Antonia could be there to stop her? All but decisively turning towards Montefort, where the one or two things she needed were, she recollected she had no money; hesitating halfway out of the woods, she beheld the Daimler—an improbable glitter far away under the shadow of the house. Maud came breathlessly up and said: "There's an answer!" (The child signalled with something blue.)

"What answer?"

Maud said: "You'll have to make up your mind."

Jane in a dream received the Latterly note; Maud, though she ostentatiously walked away, brushing off from her fingers the whole matter, more than once looked over her shoulder—Jane, it seemed, did not know how to read, or even what she should do instead. The girl did at last address herself to the bold blue page —she was wanted for dinner, dinner tonight. She thought: "Yes, but what shall I wear?"

"*THIS* has been wonderful of you," said Lady Latterly. Turning on her stool at the dressing-table, she clawed the air in the direction of Jane's hand. "Sit anywhere, then we can soon talk."

"How quickly you've cleared up after the Fête," observed Jane, gazing out at the castle lawns.

"I pay all these men; why should they not work?"

"Still, it was kind of you sending the car twice."

"You were not on the telephone; you had no car," pointed out Lady Latterly in an unresigned tone.

"We have a car, but it had gone to the sea."

"Oh. You have a house at the sea?"

"No."

"What a bother for you," remarked her new friend, busy unlocking a jewel case.

Jane went on: "Yesterday feels like years ago."

"Don't speak of it!" With a dart like a jackdaw Lady Latterly found an emerald ring, forced it on, made it

84

flash undecidedly, tore it off. She shuddered: "Never again!"

"Oh? Everybody enjoyed it."

"Who *are* all these people? What do they think I am?"

"You don't hunt yourself?"

"Not only should I be terrified, but I've a thing for foxes."

"I wonder what you do in the winter, then?"

"I don't; it couldn't be simpler. I go away."

Jane introspectively said: "I have not been here in winter for ages either."

"Oh, so that's where you've always been, is it—not here? Why has nobody told me you existed?"

"I don't expect it's very generally known."

"You go racing, surely? Why have I never seen you?"

"I imagine because I am never there."

"You ought to do something about that," said Lady Latterly, abstractedly leaning forward to view her make-up foreshortened inside the triple glass. She reapplied mascara—in a wrapper she sat with her back to Jane.

So many hours of the girl's life had already gone by in women's bedrooms that Jane, on being shown up here, felt a touch of mutiny. Not for this had she come. She would have liked to wait downstairs in the drawing-room whose theatrical emptiness had been glimpsed through an open door as she was conducted past it. However, with every possible grace she first sat down on the edge of, later reclined across, the lustrous oyster quilt of the vibrant low bed, in an attitude of compliant ease. Here, it was true, the scene was differently set—no smears, no ash, no feathers on the floor; instead, whole areas of undinted satin, no trace of anything having been touched or used. Here and there only, footprints like tracks in dew disturbed the bloom of the silver carpet. Here, supposed Jane, courteously looking round, must be a replica, priceless these days, of a Mayfair *décor* back in the 1930's—apparently still lived in without a tremor. Fancy, to know so little when one could spend so much! The necessity, the fragility, and perhaps the pathos of all this as a carapace did not strike the young girl. The bedroom gained still more unreality by now seeming trapped somewhere between day and night —this marvel of marbling and mirror-topping, mirror-building-in and prismatic whatnots being at the moment a battleground of clashing dazzling reflections and refractions. Crystal the chandelier dripped into the sunset; tense little lit lamps under peach shades were easily floated in upon by the gold of evening. Day had not done with the world yet; trees were in the conspiracy. The outdoors, light-shot, uncannily deepening without darkening, leaned through the too large windows—a blinding ray presently splintered over the dressing-table. With a cry, Lady Latterly downed tools.

"I can't see myself, you see! I can't see a thing!"

"Oh, I expect it will pass off."

"Any moment, these bastards will be arriving!"

Jane asked: "Is it a large party?"

"Eight or ten; it depends if some of them come." Lady Latterly rose, cast away her wrapper, and, in little else, stood vibrating as though with an engine running.

"I could help," said the girl, "if I knew where anything was."

"That is so, so sweet of you, but I've no idea." She set off on a lonely expedition to a hanging closet, and came back dragging a chiffon dress. "No notion how to get *into* this: my maid's gone."

"Forever?"

"Yes, couldn't stand the country. None of these people have any hearts."

"I thought your butler looked kind."

"He's going."

It was about two years since Lady Latterly had bought this unusually banal Irish castle, long empty owing to disrepair. Rumours which had preceded her into the country had not yet by any means died down, and were unlikely to. She was raven-haired, handsome, haunted—nobody could be certain by quite what. Her trials, since she took up residence here, had been not less interesting than her reputed fortune—the number of baths she had had installed under dry tanks, the lovers said or servants known to have left her, the failure of her house-parties to arrive or, still worse, leave again, the costly fiasco of her herbaceous border, the delays, non-deliveries, breakages, leakages, and general exploitation she had endured lost nothing in telling except sympathy for her: one is as rich as that at one's own risk. She was *nouveau riche*; but, as Antonia said, better late than never.

But if she chose to make history out of her vicissitudes, that was really from vauntingness—nothing beat her; she had a way of worsting one. Now she was cunningly finding her way into her own dress; and as the yards upon yards of sun-coloured chiffon perfectly fell into place around the hostess, leaving her only to make negligent play with a few loops, Jane's spirits mounted: this *was* what one had come for! For the girl tonight was in a mood for the theatre, and for that only—what else, as a finale to her inconceivable day, was to be endured? Here she was, spirited out of Montefort into this foreign dimension of the castle, in which nothing, no one, could be unreal enough.

As to that, Lady Latterly finally put together satisfied all requirements. Soaring over the chiffon, her neck, arms, shoulders seemed to be made of plastic, pure of humanity. Her face by being worn tilted back brought the more into notice a flawless jawline, which her eyes, turning down under varnished lids, would have contemplated were it but in their view. She had taken on again yesterday afternoon's air of commanding nonchalance. Satiety was in her attitude as, having billowed back to the dressing-table, she used the scent spray; and as she turned her head this way, that way, clipping on earrings, she had to let out a little sigh—she had more even of breath than she could do with. Imperviously, together with Jane, she heard car after car come up the avenue, make a scrunching turn on the gravel, stop. Guests, fresh to the evening, greeted each other in daylight out on the castle steps.

"Do go down, and say I'll be down. Amuse them."

"They will not know who I am."

"That will amuse them."

Jane entered a drawingroom black-and-white at the door end with standing men. As she advanced towards them the sound-track stopped. Bowers of flowers cascaded fern mist from the piano top; jaded late green heat came in at the open windows. The room, more quenched, less dazzling than that above by being a minute further towards nightfall, was overcast by the outdoor rise of lawns and encased in walls of transparent blue. Brought to a standstill under all these eyes by the slight shock of the sense of her own beauty, Jane said: "Lady Latterly will be late," for the first time wondering why. A woman, the apparently only other, diagonal in a black dress on a white sofa, nodded tardily at her over a picture paper, then took a cigarette out of a box—

scoffingly, she had lighted it for herself before the group had so far collected its wits as to break ranks. Who knew where they had all come from? The girl, at the advantage of being less surprised by them than they were by her, detachedly heard the silence break up into a clash of experimental, isolated remarks. She had no way of identifying the male speakers, nor did she try to—she looked from face to face, with her lips apart, uncertain as to whom to award the golden apple of her attention.

The fact was not only that she distinguished no one but that, so far, so compact was the group that all these alike, anonymous masks seemed to be attached to the same body, one abstract shirtfront. Yet she was somehow edified, already partly won, for about this composite there was something legendary—here, she was in the presence of a race she did not know yet, yet somehow knew of. Veterans in experience of their own kind, they made her feel an aggregate of maturity, of assimilated well-being, and of a vigour rather the more marked by being a little on the decline. She took them to be men of the world—what world might be left to be of, she did not ask herself. Some, perhaps, she had seen at the Fête, some not. None were young; one or two stood out as older than others—and one now again stood out by strolling away, by proclaiming himself subtly at home in this house, where the rest were nothing more than at ease, by a proprietary move to the tray of drinks. Jane had to suppose this must be in order—from the others' rather striking lack of expression, evidently it was, but was so for a reason they would have preferred the girl not to comprehend. Perturbed, she could but watch the decanter being so masterfully unstoppered—till, to divert what might be her waking thoughts, someone near her spoke up. So, he said, she was staying here?

"Oh, no. I live near here."

"Is that really so? Far from here?"

"Everywhere's far from here," she said, elatedly taking in the fictitious room.

"Round here, you know, that seems to be true of everywhere. All the same, it's extraordinary how one gets about."

Jane had, rather naturally, not thought of that: she was wondering how to be candid but not aloof when Lady Latterly, having come swishing in at the door behind her with no warning other than displaced air, swept an arm round her waist. The embrace, though intended chiefly to strike a note, was at first startling: the girl, inside the tightening arm, found herself being pivoted this way, that way, while the hostess waved round the company with her other hand. Greeting was thus very cleverly sunk in showmanship—Lady Latterly was either defying them to have seen enough of Jane, or inviting them to look at the girl again in the new and entrancing relationship she had with her. Loathing of the beginning of a party caused her, each time, to hit upon some device—and tonight, her triumphing air asked, what could one have hit upon that was better? "Tommy, Mamie, Tipps, Fitz, Terence!" she called, "isn't *this* lovely?" And she beat a tattoo upon Jane's ribs, more to keep the girl silent than make her speak. "Where did I find her? *Ah!*" Then: "Have you told them yet who you are?" she asked, just not entangling an earring in Jane's hair. "I expect not."

Lastly, she swung the girl and herself right round, to face upon the man who was acting host. The tray was some way away down the room: in step, in Siamese close-ness, they paced towards it. Ice was being made rattle in her shaker: he paused, but only in order to say nothing, which he did with what might or might not be consid-ered enough eloquence. An indecisive engagement be-tween two pairs of eyes took place, and took up enough time to make Jane, held like a ventriloquist's doll, wonder whether she could indeed be expected to be a mouthpiece—if so, Lady Latterly was let down. Lady Latterly finally said: "Why, hullo," in a voice of modu-lated surprise at having come upon him, of all people, here, or indeed anywhere in the world at all. She then told Jane: "This is my barman." His experienced wrist went back to work: they looked on—yellow chiffon fall-ing against the yellowed muslin. (Jane wore the morn-ing's dress, skirts pressed, top hastily cut out and sleeves away, for she had nothing better with her at Montefort.) Lady Latterly, braced against the fortification of Jane's body, was able to be at her most impervious—airily stretching her whipcord throat up, she brought the whole of the fearlessness with which she could be forty into display next this young country beauty. He, meanwhile, unscrewed the top of the shaker.

"Peregrine, you think those *are* dry enough?"

"They're the same as last time."

"They never have been, darling. Oh, well. For me, then; and one for Jane."

"And there'll be Mamie," he said, with a glance at the sofa.

"Why, yes, the poor thirsty thing! You must make a whole lot more, then. Once again, do you notice, no one has brought Priscilla?"

"Unless you hate a martini?" he interposed, handing Jane a glass.

"They are the end to her, really," mused Lady Latterly. She released Jane in order to take a cocktail, with which she started to walk away. "If she wants to know," she said back over her shoulder, "you might tell Jane who everyone is."

If this *was* behaviour, one had yet to learn how to deal with it. Radiant foolhardiness was not going to carry one all the way—for one thing, gone was the magical aid of sunset: impassive electric candelabra sprang into brilliance round all the eggshell walls, and by their light Jane, instinctively looking down, saw these indelible ancient grass-stains betraying the embroidered hems of her muslin; which, till now not more than gracefully long for her, lapped on the parquet limply in an exposed way. Top to toe, she was being speculated upon, however abstractedly or politely, by Peregrine, with whom she'd been left alone—momentarily, the misery of being thought artistic (for he would be sure to arrive at that) made Jane flush. She saw what it could be to lose nerve, and at the same time heard Antonia laughing. "You're nothing," she thought of the company, "but a pack of cards!"—but the cards were stacked, and against her. The evening reeked of expense: everything cost, nothing was for nothing—Lady Latterly calculated the pretty penny, and everybody was being kept hard at it paying up. Nor did "everybody" exclude Jane, who was paying by being the lovely nobody, exhibited but not introduced. Seeing this—in fact, on the whole stimulated because she saw it—she still was not sorry she had come. Let them take the consequences.

She had never drunk, only watched drinkers: inexpertly she stood holding the glass. With slow recklessness she raised the potion to her lips. The drink touched her lips, then began to go down well; she could soon amuse herself by rolling round the damp olive in empty mistiness. Glad to be disembarrassed of the martini, and at how small pains, she smiled as she handed him back the glass. "You needn't tell me who anyone is; it doesn't matter."

"No?" he said, disconcerted. "No, I suppose not, really."

"Oh, I expect it could," she conceded, looking at him kindly.

"Vesta," he said in extenuation, "is still a trifle scatty after the Fête. She rather let herself in for that. It was quite a thing for her."

"I remember fêtes at this castle when there was no one here."

"This place," he said, looking up at the ceiling, round the walls, and even out of a window for Jane's benefit, "I imagine, must have seen many changes."

"Yes, it has. No one has stayed here long."

"Let me give you another?" he said hastily.

"Yes, thank you. The olive will do again."

"Old Terence, there—if you won't object to my telling you who he is?—remembers this place in the former gay days."

"Which?" asked Jane, on the point of making a now experienced movement of glass to lips.

"Quite a time, I'm afraid, before *you* were thought of!"

"That would be true of any gay days," she said composedly. "But which?"

"Oh, you know; before it was 1914."

"Which is Terence?" Having been shown, she walked away, carrying the cocktail.

This time she came not so much towards the others as at them, with all the boringness of her youth. As a sensation, they had already had her: had she been a merely beautiful girl, she could have been mortified by being simply the same dish come round twice—as it was, as implacably making a place for herself among them she sat down, she knew how far that was, or was soon to be, from the truth. She had invaded an open-yet-closed half-circle, orientated, by the habit of this country, towards the fireplace: tonight, because of the heat wave the grate was empty—in view of which, or rather to escape from the view of which, Lady Latterly would have done well to rearrange the room, but had not thought of it. The men, abandoning the certain loftiness they had had while standing, had lowered themselves—in all senses, Jane considered—into deep chairs; which rendered them, whether or not they liked this, almost supine before Lady Latterly and Mamie. For those two sat rearing spirally up, one at each end of the sofa once Mamie's only, each with her spine supporting a stack of cushions. Clearly there would be no notion of dinner till glasses had been refilled many times more—hard at it, the party were contradicting each other, some with passion, some with dogged authority, on a subject of which Jane

understood little but that it had ceased to be the quite
same for them all. A somewhat hopeless move to let the
girl in, on the part of the man who had taken it she was
staying here, and in spite of everything still did so, was
overruled by the others by closing ranks, and still more
was discountenanced by the girl herself. For upon her
other hand was old Terence.

She drank; then, keeping the stem of her emptied
glass in balance between her two longest fingers, took
advantage of solitude to study him. Only native other
than Jane here, her neighbour reacted to her telepathy
with a sort of uneasy, dodging, delaying half-glance out
of the corners of his wetly bright, too blue eyes. Alcohol,
though he had a famous head, so quickly brought to the
surface his Irish birthmarks that, even by this stage of
the evening, one no longer could have mistaken him for
the others—indeed how, it was to be wondered, could
the girl have done so even at first? From the being out
to the skin he was more florid. His exaggeration of his
bravado, his brogue, himself, was less exactly deliberate
than he fancied—how much was acting, how much second nature? Vanity, guilt, and sentimentality were at
work in him, undiagnosed yet worked upon by the
aliens. Bad enough having got himself in with this set
without being detected by God's spy. "Hey!" he said,
"what d'you look at me for?"

"Only, I wonder what you remember."

Terence behaved like an old boy by attempting to beetle at her with one eyebrow, in an automatic, "wait-till-you're married" way. He then announced: "The trouble is, I'm an old man."

"That's why I—" She stopped, she hoped, just in time. Terence, not having listened, did not take umbrage—chiefly, her anxious pause made him hope he had checked her, might yet give her the slip. He trailed his eye away, let it be caught elsewhere, and did the best he could to appear gone. Jane, however, soon gently re-called him. "Can you, for instance, remember this house?"

"Why would I want to remember it, when I'm sitting here?"

"Years ago, I mean."

Terence, leaning her way confidentially, said: "Now don't *you* start having me on too, there's a dear good girl. By now there are too many years ago, and I'm getting sick to death of the whole bang lot of them—rotten old romancing and story-telling: you make the half of it up, and who's the wiser? What does it matter, anyway?— Yes, I daresay," he had to add, with a gleam of lust, not for her, "I *could* make you sit up, but then again I might not: nothing's much to any of you these days—is it now?" he asked, suspicious, measuring her. "You can buy up a lot; you can't buy the past. What is it?—not even history. Goes to dust in your hand."

"I don't buy," she said, "I have no money. Do you remember Montefort?"

"Montefort? Pity that place has gone."

"But I live there."

"Good God. What are you doing here, then?"

"I was asked."

"She's a wonder," quoth Terence, dallying with his tumbler, satirically thumbing the new cut glass. "And you—fish out of water, or not, eh?"

She only smiled and swept back her gold hair, as though by showing more of her face to show how little she had to fear from anyone—but the gesture, as answer, was unconscious. She continued: "You were at Montefort?"

"Why not? That is to say, at one time."

"When?"

"Now you tell me this: who's your father?"

She told him. None the wiser, trying hard not to show it, he hazarded: "I ever buy a horse off him?"

She said impatiently: "No, I don't suppose so."

"Well, I understood that place had got into farmers' hands?"

"Well, it has."

He took another look at her.

"*When* were you most at Montefort?"

At that, Terence banged down his tumbler and menaced Jane with the palm of a raised hand—he had the

right to give her a sound slap, in default of which he
smote an arm of his chair. "Now it's no use trying to pin
me down! When I say 'one time,' I mean the time I
mean, and that's good enough." He blustered away at
her: "I'm my own calendar." Then his tone changed.
"Though I don't mind telling you this—" He looked
warily round them, then leaned towards her: his features
twitched. "These days, one goes where the money is—
with all due respect to this charming lady. Those days,
we went where the people were."

She drew a profound breath. "My cousin Guy—"

But Peregrine stood over her with the shaker; Jane
held up her glass to be once more filled—at which
Mamie could not but pop her eyes. "These are power-
ful, you know—or perhaps you don't know?" she called
across, direly waving the drink of which she spoke as
she re-scrambled for balance among the cushions. Jane
glanced at Mamie's pomegranate toenails, curling out
of a sandal, but said nothing: the contents of the glass,
which sip by sip became the contents of her, had no
bearing whatever upon the situation that she could see.
She experienced the absolute calmness, the sense of there
being almost no threat at all, with which one could
imagine fighting one's way down a burning staircase—
there *was* a licking danger, but not to her; cool she
moved down between flame walls. Only, all went to
heighten her striking power—and had she not struck

when she spoke the name! It had left her lips and was in the room.

Guy was among them. The recoil of the others—she did not for an instant doubt it *was* a recoil—marked his triumphant displacement of their air. She saw the reflection of crisis in each face, heard it in loudening, dropping, then stopping voices. Dinner had been announced; but it was not, could not be simply that—the butler vanishing from the door had no more than offered an alibi or afforded cover for a single, concerted movement of disarray on the part of these poor ghosts on whom the sun had risen, to whom the cock crew. Lady Latterly moaned as she stood up; dissolution flowed through the chiffon and her limbs as she linked what was left of an arm through dissolving Mamie's. Jane herself rose, stood, the better to enjoy the spectacle of the flight, the glissade of the shadow-show, the enforced retreat from here to nowhere—but herself was caught in the mist of their thinning semblances. She tottered, was thankful to find her hand ensconced on the chimneypiece of eternal marble. She was right; there *was* one more figure among the men—all knew this; what were they waiting for?

Or might no man move till she raised the spell?

Lady Latterly, turning round in the doorway, said: "Jane, my sweet, I *think* men want to come in to dinner! . . . What can you mean, Mamie?" she murmured, aside, askance. She billowed back in her tracks and scooped up the girl: three abreast, the ladies entered the diningroom.

"Why do I never have a butler who can count?" asked Lady Latterly, indicating, when they had all sat down, an empty place, laid, and an empty chair. "Oh, no, though, I forgot: that was for Priscilla.—No, leave it, Duffy; but *do,* another time, count!"

"Are you sure he thought it was for Priscilla?"

"What can you mean?"

"Oh, nothing."

"Oh, I do hate your manner: don't be occult!"

"Why are you having it left, then?"

"What, that place? Because it was for Priscilla. To make you sorry."

"As a matter of fact, Vesta, you never asked her."

"Oh, that's so, so untrue!"

"Well, so Priscilla says."

Peregrine interposed: "I know there's a castle in this country where an extra place is laid every night for dinner. It's in some way connected with the family curse."

"How do *you* know?"

Peregrine lost heart. "You had a banshee, Terence?" he said hopelessly.

Terence, one side of the empty place, edged his chair first confidentially in to, then uneasily outward again from it; then began to spoon up liquidly-jellied madrilene at a great rate. The man on the other side found himself with no alternative to Mamie. She, however, was busily reaching out, pulling out a rose from the centre bowl; leaning across her neighbour, she dropped the rose between the knives and forks of the empty place, saying: "*There,* darling! You're my ideal man." In the following pause the rest of the roses, outraged and candle-scorched, began to shed petals over the salted almonds. Seated across the table, which was a round one, Jane faced the gap in the ring of lit-up masks.

"Duffy," said Lady Latterly, "take the roses away. They look second-hand."

"Really, Vesta."

"Well, Mamie keeps on awarding them."

"Only one," said Jane, who was seen to smile.

"Well, I can't stand Mamie being Lady Macbeth."

"No," Peregrine said, "you've got this all mixed up with Ophelia."

"Oh, well, Ophelia; just as you like. I suppose you know Ophelia was raving mad?"

Mamie, hauling a velvet strap up a fat white shoulder, said: "All I know is, I did a beautiful thing."

Jane gave her the half-smile again.

Darkness rose to a height in the corners of the room; there were dimmed lamps over the serving-tables. Uncurtained windows stood open; breathless seemed the night, yet now and then a tremor ran through the candles, each time causing a shadowed contraction of all faces. An owl was to be heard back in the woods; and the Irish butler, moving about, gave the impression of harkening for something more. Guy had dined here often.

A moth sheered the candles and fell scorched on to Mamie's rose—at which Terence's eyes consulted Jane's; unostentatiously putting a hand out, he pinched the moth to death. Talk, which zigzagged up to a pitch, stopped: everyone was aware of the old assassin wiping his fingers off on the sheeny napkin. The girl's odd bridal ascendancy over the dinner table, which had begun to be sensed since they sat down, declared itself—*she* was the authority for the slaying. Tolerating the tribute of the rose, she could not suffer dyingness to usurp: she let out a breath as the moth was brushed from the cloth. That done, she was withheld again. Her dilated oblique glances, her preoccupation less with eating and drinking than with glasses and forks, gave her the look of some-one always abstaining from looking across too speakingly at a lover—not a soul failed to feel the electric connec-tion between Jane's paleness and the dark of the chair in which so far no one visibly sat. Between them, the two dominated the party.

Or, so they acted on barbarian nerves. In this particu-lar company, by this time of the evening, even counter-feit notions of reality had begun to wobble. Who knew,

who could not compute, to a man, exactly how many
sat round the table? The evening offered footing to the
peculiar by being itself out of the true—there was something phantasmagoric about this circle of the displaced
rich. Reason annihilated itself when these people met.
Together, they pressed themselves and each other to the
extreme limits of their faculties: beyond what they were
capable of lay what? They had warped their wits with
disproportionate stories; at any turn the preposterous
might lay final claim on them—there was no censor.
Even Shakespeare had stalked in. He and drink played
havoc with known dimensions. There was a stir if not a
kindling of exhausted senses, only now to be heated by
being haunted; between the sexes there lingered on an
amorous animosity, far spent. Mood had been dipping
towards a vacuum; the camp lights sank—outside waited
the stilly night. Had they been imaginative, had so much
as one of them been a person at any other instant aware
or keyed up, they would together have made less apt
conductors: as it was, the current made circuit through
them. Something more peremptory, more unfettered
than imagination did now command them—there *had*
been an entrance, though they could not say when.

The men, within an inch of being outmanned, rallied.
Mamie, having for some time given the impression that
she had shot her bolt by that inspirational doing with
the rose, sat up and took rather cosmic notice. Lady Lat-

terly leaned across and, with the back of her fingers, delivered a flick or knock at Peregrine's wrist—negatively
seated beside Jane, he had scooped up petals and out of
them had been composing a hieroglyphic on the lace
cloth, for his own silently whistling and slightly frowning attention only. With a start, he acknowledged her
taloned hand. The galante revival was signalized by a
lifting of glasses, almost as though to drink a toast; and
though one by one these were put down again, there
remained the sensation that there had been a moment.
There ensued a release of ardour and flattery, so that
the two women, though set always back from the spot-
lit Jane, could each queen it over new little subsidiary
courts of love. In its own way, talk took a heroic turn—
a recollection of action as it could be, a glint of authority
through bravery, a look of being back again on the met-
tle, appeared on faces, making them less acquiescent and
less opaque; it now was possible, looking round, to distinguish each man from the others by the revivification
of some unequivocal quality he and he only had had
when young. At the same time, while these men helped
to compose Guy, they remained tributary to him and
less real to Jane—that is, as embodiments—than was he.

Snapshots taken before Antonia was a photographer
fused with the "studio portrait" taken in uniform for
Lilia, on the hall wall at Montefort (oak-framed, overcast by the flank of the stopped clock, all but secretively

to be disregarded) and with what was inadvertently still
more photographic in shreds of talk. Over the combina-
tion of glance and feature, the suggestion of latitude in
the smile, rested a sort of indolent sweet force. Now
more than living, this face had acquired a brightened
cast of its own from the semi-darkness, from which it
looked out with an easy conviction of being recognized.
Nothing was qualified or momentary about it, as in the
pictures; this was the face of someone here to the full—
visible, and visible all at once, were the variations and
contradictions, the lights and shades of the arrested tor-
rent of an existence. Invisibly concentrated around him
was all the time he had ever breathed: his todays, his
yesterdays, his anticipated tomorrows—it could be felt
how and understood why something had emanated from
him so strongly into the experience of the room when he
joined the party. The set of his head was joyous and dic-
tatorial—he was *at* the party, into it, key-placed in the
zonal merging manly pattern of black-and-white round
this round table. What yet was to be recognized was his
voice—so expectant of it that she kept on all but de-
tecting it, just not here or there, just not now or then
but at the same time everywhere and always, in extrane-
ous overrising or underlying notes, tones, syllables, mod-
ulations in the now crowded vociferous general talk,
Jane sat listening for it and to no other. She could not
but know it when once she heard it, could not but hear

it since it was to be heard, it could not but be to be heard since it would not be like him not to be talking. What remained beyond her was what he said—she had not the wits, at the moment, to take it in, even if it was to be sorted out. Her absorption—as from time to time, without raising her eyes, she recollected a glass and again drank from it or, putting out what seemed no longer to be exactly her own hand, played with a petal between her plate and Peregrine's—was solely in her sense of his being *here*. Here he is, because this is where I am. He had come to join her—join her, and on the strength of one invocation of his name! Before speaking it, had not the breath she drew been big with risk and exhilaration? The sound had gone out on to knowing air: had not the moment suffered as, with a shock, it took the charge of immanence and fatality? . . . And now? She must hope never in all her life again to be so aware of him, or indeed of anyone—for this was becoming so much too much for Jane, so giddying, as to be within an iota of being nothing. The annihilation-point of sensation came into view, as something she was beginning to long to reach. She began to wonder how it would be to look straight across the table. For, what continued to tell her that he was there dinned in the knowing of why and how. Dominator of the margin of the vision, he was all the time the creature of extra sense. The face depended for being there upon there being no instant when it was looked straight at.

So the resemblances to Antonia became more haunting because they could not be scrutinized. It was as though he, to speed up the coming back, carelessly had annexed from the cousin he counted sister some traits of hers, and was at once making use of them and subduing them. Or could it be that Antonia, left alone, had consoled or rebuilt herself by copying Guy, and that one now was in the presence of the original? The resemblance, nothing to do with feature, had come out in none of the photographs of Guy: it was an affair of mobility, of livingness—something to do, perhaps, with an interlock between the cousins' two ways of being, apart, yet one the cause of the other. Neither could be in abeyance while the other lived: he now tonight recalled Antonia, as she must often (had one known what was happening) have recalled him. His tenancy of her perhaps accounted for the restless mannishness in the woman she was—and yet, no: for all her accesses of womanishness, one could make a guess at the man she would have been, and it would have been a different man, not Guy. This was a question of close alikeness (with everything psychic, emotional, perhaps fatal which such alikeness could comprehend), not, for an instant, of identity. That the likeness should be a matter of look not looks, that it less declared than betrayed itself, like a secret history, made a deep-down factor of it—not least for Jane. The effect on her was to create a fresh significance for Antonia.

Torment caused the girl to look straight across.

He was gone. To mark this, at the same moment Terence, swaying sideways to give force to an argument, leaned a hand on the back of the empty chair. It was to be noted—and Jane did note, for she stared hard at it— how characteristic the old fellow's turned-up thumb was. Below it was gleaming, to her relief, the unhidden Chinese Chippendale pattern of the mahogany. She was free to entertain joy as not before: indeed she saw Guy now that she saw him gone. Not a vestige stayed on the outer air; she could therefore enter the full of seeing and knowing. That he had been with them, with her, was an unfettered fact—where is there perfection but in the memory?

The candles were burning some way down. How late was it? With lassitude a clock once again struck.

"*I* don't say so," Mamie was saying, "Priscilla says so."

"Then heaven help her," Terence was saying, "the woman's wrong. The horse was looking at me last Friday."

"Oh, well, it will be all the same a hundred years hence, I daresay."

"Now there you're wrong: you won't find a horse left."

Mamie yawned: "What dreadful things you say." She stretched out, reclaimed the rose, and tucked it into the tight top of her dress.

"Mamie won't even be there to find no horses," said Peregrine, rousing himself suddenly. "You might just be there," he added, turning to Jane, "but shrivelled up like a monkey, with black teeth. So why don't you make hay while the sun shines?"

She replied: "I was making hay this morning."

"Ah, then that *is* a hayseed in your hair.—May I?" Peregrine picked it out. "How literal of you," he said sadly, placing the seed on the cloth for Jane to study.

"Hello," said Lady Latterly, "what have you both got there?—What is it *now?*" she snapped at the butler, who had come and was waiting by her chair.

"If you please, m'lady, the young lady's cousin has come for her."

"Why, when? Who's the young lady's cousin?"

"She gave no name."

"Well, then, bring her in then, for heaven's sake!"

"She'd prefer, she said, to stop at the door."

"How very, very peculiar," said Lady Latterly.

ANTONIA backed the Ford clear of other cars, snatched her gear out again from reverse, and tore rocketing off round the gravel sweep. Jane, looking back at the castle, to which lighted windows and butler still on the steps gave a farewell theatricality, observed: "We seem to be going away with an awful noise."

"And how had you been thinking of getting home?"

"No one was going away yet."

"Have you any idea what time it is?"

"No," said the girl indifferently. "Why, have you?" Their headlights ran extra sharply over the rhododendrons lining the avenue—a rabbit shot out, swirled in the glare, and vanished under the wheels. Antonia, swerving too late, swore. Jane, pursuing what seemed the line of thought, went on: "You mean, you were late at the sea?"

"Not at all," said Antonia sea-coldly.

"Then if it isn't late, why did you come for me so early? What made you come for me at all?"

"I thought it likely you'd be what indeed you are."

"What indeed am I?"

"Drunk, you little bore."

"Not necessarily," said Jane in an even tone. "One can be other things than that." Reflectively she waited to let the car turn out of the castellated gateway, then said: "I don't a bit feel like you sometimes seem."

"That is no guide at all, I assure you."

"I simply feel I'm more than just simply me."

"You'll soon get to recognize that sensation. All the same," stormed Antonia, "what a way to start! What a seedy outing! And you were seduced also, I daresay?"

"Oh, no; we sat in the drawingroom, then in the diningroom. Everyone she'd invited was quite old."

"What d'you mean, 'everyone she'd invited'?—Anyone crash the party?"

The girl was silent.

Antonia repeated: "A seedy outing!"

Jane said mildly: "It was an evening out."

"Rats: it was a get-away." Antonia jerked the car to a stop, for the aggressive purpose of lighting the cigarette she was in no mood to let Jane light for her; she did indeed, by the at once alcoholic and slighting over-precision of her own movements, imply she considered Jane in no state to do so. The burning match cast out through the wound-down window was on its way followed by Jane's eyes—so, realized the girl, smelling bracken char-

ring where it had fallen, so long as there's fuel there's no
extinction! Engine running, the Ford was pulled up half
in the ditch and canting towards the hedge, whose secre-
tive night-scents whispered to the senses with their
"again." Jane, folding cooled arms across her breast to
hug in her heart, confided: *"This* was the road, last
night."

Antonia with irony said: "Extraordinary."

"Which is why I wish you'd leave me alone."

"I can hardly wait to. Walk home, by all means!"

"Don't be furious," pleaded the girl. "I am so happy."

"I can't help that."

"Is that why you are furious?"

Antonia turned in the driver's seat to accord Jane a
brief, contemptuous stare, intensified by the dark between them. "I forget," she said, "how ordinary you are.
For that, I should blame nobody but myself."

"Not me, then, for going to the castle?"

"What, for running to where you're whistled for,
nipping off the moment my back was turned? I could
hardly be madder with you, I'm bound to say."

"But you were furious before that. After all, you went
to the sea without me."

"The sea without you is sometimes nice." Antonia
stamped her foot down and they moved on again, as
though something had been established, which it had

not. Jane's ecstatic willingness to be silent became as in-sistent as though the girl were singing—suspicion that inwardly she was, and a tormented refusal to know why, preyed on Antonia as the night jolted past them. The swerving course of the Ford made honeysuckle, a boot caught on the hedge, the cadaverous chimney-end of a vanished cottage, a hallucinated wandering white horse, lurch out, from one side then the other, into glaring view: their way seemed to be posted along with warn-ings, in spite of which Antonia spoke and said: "This road *I* knew before you were born."

"Oh. Was there always that white horse?"

"Why?"

"Only, I think we drove right through it."

"Who was there, tonight?" Antonia suddenly asked, matching a change of gear with a change of tone.

Jane glanced the driver's way. "There was old Ter-ence."

"Not Terence Foxe—still going?"

"Yes, in a way. I forgot to ask him if he remembered you."

"Why should you ask him if he remembered me?"

"Because I asked him if he remembered Guy."

"You don't ask me if I remember Guy."

"Ask you—why should I? How could you not?"

"Me? I not only *could* not, it's a question whether I

ever do. You, Jane, can't conceive what memory is. You can't conceive what memory costs. Remember? Who could afford to?"

"Mother affords to."

"Yes, and easily too. The long and short of it, you're your mother's daughter."

"Antonia—*was* he in love with her?"

"Who, Guy?"

"Oh, you well know who we're talking about!"

"Yes, I do; but you don't, or you couldn't ask such an unmeaning question. The whole of a man!"

"I know," asserted the girl.

"Believe what you like," cried Antonia. "He's dead and out of it."

"You sound as though you were thanking God."

"No, I don't think I am—why?"

"Antonia, it was Guy who was there tonight."

"He always had rotten taste in company.—Well, go on, get out, open the gate!"

"Why, *are* we here?"

"Apparently," said Antonia.

They were. The Ford, knowingly slowing down, pulled up nose in to the warped white spears and chain knot of the Montefort entrance—the eating-out of rust through the last paint gave the gates, analyzed by the headlights, more than their daytime aspect of dissolution: could they not be driven through like the horse?

Obediently clambering out in her long skirts, Jane declared: "I still am not what you think." Shock, nevertheless, made her hands shake, mismanaging, so that the knot of links only tightened upon itself; and while she fumbled away at it, watched by Antonia, she was impaled as the victim of a scorn which made her lower her head and shrink in her shoulders. Gates once open, Antonia shot through them and straight on, away down the avenue, leaving Jane to stare after the wobbling tail-light. She pulled to the gates and made fast the chain again in the dark.

At Montefort, Fred was still about—in the hall he had taken the chimney off the low-burning oil lamp on the table and was digging at the wick with his pocket-knife. Antonia, having put the car away, came through from the yard by the back door at the same moment as Jane came in at the front. He wiped the blade and closed it— just in time, for his daughter ran straight to him, put her arms round him and her face to be kissed, and remained there breathless in his astonished hold. "Steady," he said, steadying them both. "Why, your heart's beating!"

"Is it?"

"Like anything," said her father.

"Are you glad I'm home?"

"Began to wonder if you'd be there all night."

"Antonia," said Antonia, "dealt with that." Unrestrainedly coughing, she shoved past them, grasped the banister rail, and started to pull herself upstairs as though to bed; but halfway up changed her mind and sat down. From up there, a nightbird over their heads, she croaked: "Such a wonderful party . . ."

"*Was* it?" Fred instantly asked Jane, to feel only, in her closeness to him, a half-movement like a submerged answer. Gathering his will together, he gave her a sort of push out of his arms, as though it was better to have her at seeing distance. Left to stand, she stood in a daze; while he, stupefied by the sweet mistake of the embrace, ran a hand down one side of his jaw and up the other, over the stubble. "Or, how was it?" he tentatively went on.

A conspiratorial turn of Jane's head towards the staircase invited him to see why she could not tell—now, at the minute, as things were. But there was a "later," a reckless impassioned promise, a look of meaning to stay till they *were* alone, about her manner of sitting down on the hall's least unsteady Gothic chair, with its pile of musty folded horse-cloths. Slipping off a sandal, she shook out of it a hurting little stone from the avenue. He asked: "How did you manage to pick that up?"

"Certainly not at the castle; it's richly carpeted."

"So it ought to be." Mind upon something else, he turned to put the chimney back on the lamp—then: "What you're wearing, what you've got on," he said, "is it new, or would it be very old? Is it that dress out of the trunk?"

"Don't you like it?"

"It makes you different, to me. But then that could be tonight, of course." He again considered her. "I don't suppose I've ever seen you before when you'd just come home from any party. So it could be that.—*Is* it the dress out of the trunk?"

"Yes. Am I different?" she asked, stooping down to put on the sandal.

All he said was: "If you had lived here more . . ."

Jane sat on giddily in the hot lamplight: on the wall behind her hung generations of coats, cloaks, mackintoshes, and she leaned her head back into them with a sigh. Her father said: "I had a glass of milk for you. Do you want it?"

Up there, Antonia's watching-and-waiting attitude, known to this staircase in whose shadows and corners she had in adolescence so often crouched, now was changed by a new activity—she began licking brine from one of her wrists. In one half of the self which had come apart she was recalling the sea as she had left it—nobody's, empty as a glass under heat mist which began to darken, tide sucking at the beach as it went out. There had been no other swimmer—none in reality. For the other half of her, what went on in the hall down there was more and more assuming a grotesque cast: there had been a race between herself and Jane into Fred's arms, and the girl had won. Antonia counted the times when he and she could have been lovers: could one continue what was never begun? Tonight the answer could have been, yes. Everything was magnified and distorted; everything had its way with the unpent senses—the stone cast from the sandal spat like a shot on the floor; the lamp chimney around the urged-on lamp flame gave warning by an ear-splitting crack, and the flame itself, spurting threads of itself and smoke stinkingly upward toward the ceiling, crimsonly stuttered inside the gloom it made like an evil tongue. Watching the scene being played out at the foot of the stairs, she saw at work in Jane, as in herself, the annihilating need left behind by Guy.

All salt from the wrist being now on tongue, Antonia allowed the wrist to drop. Instinctively turning, peering into the shadow between the banisters, she tried to fix whether, as a fact or not, the scene had a witness other than her—there, on the dark side of the projecting clock, ought to hang (and had certainly hung for years) the military photograph of Guy. One remembered its having been in position. How lately? Why should it not have fallen the last time plaster fell from the wall? If so, no one had said so—but who would ever say so, say so to her, when *her* sole recognition of the thing had been, from the outset, of an enormity? . . . Was he, all

the same, looking on now?—Fred thickly cut across her
line of vision; on his way through to the kitchen for the
milk he passed between the banisters and the wall, followed almost immediately by a Jane unwilling to be left
either behind him or near Antonia. Antonia, loth to
have them out of her sight, still more so to be in sight
of no one, got up and came down to follow the two. But
it was the front door, left wide open upon the allaying
night, which instead drew her.

Drawn she was, all but knowing why. Going to stand
in the doorway, she was met at once by a windlike rushing towards her out of the dark—her youth and Guy's,
from every direction: the obelisk, avenue, wide country, steep woods, river below. No part of the night was
not breathless breathing, no part of the quickened stillness not running feet. A call or calling, now near by, now
from behind the skyline, was unlocatable as a corn-
crake's in uncut grass. A rising this was, on the part of
two who like hundreds seemed to be teeming over the
land, carrying all before them. The night, ridden by
pure excitement, was seized by hope. All round Montefort there was going forward an entering back again into
possession: the two, now one again, were again here—
only the water of their moments had run away long since
along the way of the river; the root-matted earthiness
and the rockiness were as ever their own, and stable. All
they had ever touched still now physically held its charge

—everything that had been stepped on, scaled up, crept under, brushed against, or leaped from now gave out, touched by so much as air, a tingling continuous sweet shock, which the air suffered as though it were half laughing, as was Antonia.

Exhilaration caught her in the lungs. Their tide had turned and was racing in again: here was the universe filling up—all there had been to be, do, know, dare, live for, or die for at the full came flooding to this doorstep. Doom was lifted from her. Moreover, all was certain: nothing could have been firmer than this doorstep on which she bodily stood (this stone which though it had cracked and sunk had cracked no wider, sunk no further) except Antonia's certainty of tonight. This was not the long-ago, it was *now* or nothing—the stink of the expiring lamp came fanning out from the hall behind her; unmistakably was her stout shadow cast forward over the little garden. Ghosts could have no place in this active darkness—more, tonight was a night which had changed hands, going back again to its lordly owners: time again was into the clutch of herself and Guy. Stamped was the hour, as were their others.

What was returned to her was the sense of "always" —the conviction of going on, on and on. His and her customary battles, ordeals, risks had been so many violent testings of immortality; nor had the two of them yet not won. They had used an unpitying roughness with one another—and yes, the brunt of that was to be felt again. What had started, when first she came to the door, as a righting and pacification of her senses had gone on to be an entire re-tuning of them. Bodily she had been left a clean slate, as it were at the start of a child's day—likely to be, and being, soon scored all over with cuts, stings, burns, bruises, grazes, and brambly flesh-tearings. Inflicted wrenchings echoed over her joints; once again she tasted the poisonberries experimentally forced between each other's lips to see whether it *was* possible to kill. What they did to each other, or at each other's expense, uncaringness kept from having been cruelty, just as unknowingness kept it from having been love. They conceived of no death, least of all death-in-life—an endless rushing, or rushing endlessness, was their domain, as it was their element. They had, by their action upon each other, generated a ceaseless energy, which accumulated in them when they did not use it—when they went blank, for instance, when they projected nothing, or when, all out, they flung themselves down into abeyances like dogs. Or, having been running, one bringing the other to a stop they would stand at attention, face to face, waiting for the signal to go on again, waiting to see from which of them it was to come —for not come it could not and never did.

That taut pause, that questioning confrontation, was again to rivet Guy and Antonia. *This* time, who gave the signal? Never had signal mattered so much—so much so that she flinched, or perhaps mistook it. "Wait, I—" she hurriedly said, aloud.

Above, Lilia came to her bedroom window. "What's the matter? Who's that you're talking to?"

"Is that *you,* Lilia?" queried Antonia, shaken.

"Yes. Why not?"

"Can't you sleep?"

"Is Jane back—everyone back?"

"Everyone's back."

"Who did you say?"

"Everyone."

"Who's that down there with you?"

"You must be dreaming!"

"Your voice sounds funny, Antonia.—You'll lock the door, then?"

"Yes. Go back to bed. Good night."

Antonia, having stepped back into the hall, lost no time in barricading the door behind her, which she did with a lightheaded willingness, going through a performance which meant nothing—forcing the key round in the stiff lock, letting drop the crossbar into its sockets. Not since Montefort stood had there ceased to be vigilant measures against the nightcomer; all being part of the hostile watch kept by now eyeless towers and time-stunted castles along these rivers. For as land knows, everywhere is a frontier; and the outposted few (and

few are the living) never must be off guard. But tonight
the ceremony became a mockery: when Antonia had
done bolting and barring she remained, arms extended
across like another crossbar, laughing at the door. For
the harsh-grained oak had gone into dissolution: it shut
out nothing. So was demolished all that had lately stood
between him and her. . . . Behind her, however, was
someone else.

Locking up the house officially was Fred's duty; having heard Antonia at it, he came to check up, halting
where, at the distant end of the hall, the archway led
from the kitchen passage. "Why—thanks!" he exclaimed.

"That's all right," she said, turning round, "you were
with a girl."

That he took bemusedly, with a love-foolish half-
laugh. Antonia's affably going on, "Quite like old
times," made him twist the grin off his mouth uncertainly, to remark no more than: "Well, that's one way
to put it."

"Jane is quite a girl."

"She's asleep," he gave out, suddenly very sternly.
"Beat out, whatever they did to her over there. You and
I'd better somehow get her to bed."

"Oh, by all means." Antonia went with Fred along
the stone way into the kitchen. On the table a candle
was burning: near it Guy's latest love, seated, had fallen

forward, cheek on her arms like a tired servant; by her
the tasted glass of milk. Antonia, not ungently putting
aside the tumble of hair, looked down: here was beauty
—never more beautiful than now in its dereliction and
with its hopeless air of forgotten promise. From where
had the girl got it, and so purely? She had ravened nothing but fairness out of her mother. "*Our* blood, his and
mine," thought Antonia, roundabout by way of the by-
blow Fred. Asleep and besotted Jane, wine on her
breath, made a point for the confluence of lost bright
forces. Antonia cried out: "She should have been his
daughter!"

The words were out—under them, Jane slept on un-
stirred. On the stove-top there sizzled drip from a kettle.
After some time: "Were you speaking to me?" Fred
asked.

"I—I am not sure," faltered Antonia.

His face wore its look of having been struck across, a
drawn-out look of amazement which not yet was either
patience or anger. He searched around and slowly picked
up a chair—Antonia recollected Lilia's conviction that
Fred had at one or another time killed a man. What he
did was to carry the chair to the table and sit down upon
it defiantly close to Jane. He drew towards him the glass
of milk and tilted it, tongue out at a corner of his mouth
as though the operation were precarious; then finally

heavily shrugged his shoulders. He muttered something inaudible.

"What?" she asked.

"What d'you mean, 'what'?" he in turn asked.

"I only couldn't hear what you said, Fred."

"I heard you all right. What am I supposed to say?"

"There's nothing *for* you to say. I should never have—"

"I'm not so sure," he said, looking at her squarely. "Not so sure there's nothing for me to say."

"Go ahead, then." Antonia, standing waiting, stuffed her fists down into her jacket pockets, till she heard one of the linings rip. Fred got the glass of milk back again into vertical on the table, then shook his head. "No. After all, what's the use?"

She could not tell him.

Fred with a frown considered the girl between them. "I always have been sorry for you, Antonia. You and I are entitled to our own thoughts; but what I do say is 'Let sleeping dogs lie.' "

"Sleeping Jane?"

"*She's* got to be got to bed." He turned his wrist to look at his watch, oppressedly. "But you know as well as I do, I don't mean her."

Antonia turned away to pace round the kitchen. At this post-midnight hour the flagged floor began to be running with cockroaches; in her course she scrunched down hard upon three or four of them. Returning, she sat herself on the table's edge, her feet swinging clear of the infestation, her torso twisted towards Fred, whom she had found the mind to address more boldly. "Or there was another answer open to you: 'A living dog's better than a dead lion.' " She took a cigarette, offered him the packet.

"Why, yes." They both lit up from the candle—he leaned back, and afterwards blew out smoke. "Why not? True enough, after all. *I'm* alive—eh?" Slowly boastful, he thumped himself on the midriff. "So what of that?" he asked the unhearing Jane.

"What of that?" marvelled Antonia. "She *is* your daughter—what more do you want?"

"I don't know," he said moodily. "The moon."

Jane, with an unwaking sigh, repillowed her head on her forearms: her coinlike profile now turned her father's way. "So did Guy," said Antonia.

"What, sleep like that?" asked Fred, watching the sleeper.

"No, want the moon."

"He all but got it, I should have thought. Lilia was a most wonderfully lovely girl."

"How do *you* know, Fred?"

He said simply: "I loved her for what she once was." Antonia could only exclaim: "Oh, Fred!"

"Well?" he said, warily looking up.

"I'm not sure it's not you who'll break my heart!" She saw the grin go up one side of his face; he paused to knock ash off his cigarette. "All right," he said, "go on, call me a sucker—all right. *I* know you made me take her; I know you thought you'd been pretty smart. Nevertheless, at the time there was more to it—for me, I mean. I mean to say, there it was—I was mad for her."

"Mad for what?"

"What I saw in her."

"Tell me, what?"

Fred said: "What he once saw—I suppose. That *was* somewhere in her—where do you think Jane came from?"

"Jane? A shower of gold."

"Never have granted Lilia anything, have you?" he said resignedly more than tauntingly. "Not that *I'd* blame jealousy—eats away like a rat in one, doesn't it? No, it's no pleasure. But whatever came over you, falling in love with him?"

"I don't know," said Antonia. "I don't know."

"Only look," Fred went on, "what you chucked away. You and he were something out of the common—looking back, I see even I saw that; though as you know I had my own fish to fry. In those days, I mean, when you, he, and I used to be knocking around this place. Naturally, we were kids then; but all the same . . . The way you two were, you could have run the world. That still was the way it was when I cleared out."

"So you did. And I mucked everything up?"

"No use asking me."

"Fred," she said, "it was not as simple as that."

"No? Good."

She said: "Guy was Guy."

"Can't say I ever knew him."

"But you remember there *was* Guy?"

Something snapped in Fred. He shouted: "God, Antonia—how can I ever not?"

He then gave a violent obsessive yawn, after which he scrubbed his face with his hands. Jane woke: stupefied by the candle, she attempted to ask them why it was not tomorrow.

VII

IN THE small hours of that night, Lilia reached a decision. She came downstairs next morning pale, as always, but steadied, another woman. "I'm going in this morning to have my hair cut." (Going in meant going in to Clonmore.) "I've made up my mind to have an amount off—much of my trouble in this heat has been due to my head having no ventilation. And we need salad-servers."

"Whatever for?"

"The salad bowl. Also I might take Maud."

"Otherwise I would drive you. I might still."

"Thanks, Antonia, really. But I thought it might be practice for Jane."

"I'd love to try," admitted the elder daughter.

The ladies were in the rampart garden, watching Kathie cutting rhubarb for dinner—one by one they had followed each other out. Here was a smell of thyme and a look of peace; the languid mountains, seen through gaps in the wall, seemed to be fainting behind gauze. Lilia, holding a cup and saucer, wore cotton of

131

an extinct blue, of a shade only less indolent than the sky's—side-by-side on a stone bench, she and Antonia were under a twisted apple tree silvered over with lichen. Jane had found a bed inside a box-edged oval; and not far off stood the sundial, around which old poppies lolled, bees dozed on the yellow lupins. Below, the river had almost ceased to run; a nonchalant stillness hung over everywhere. It was thought to be about eleven o'clock.

The three were becalmed by each other. Somehow it had happened that they had fallen into one of those dilatory patterns of country-house life little known these days to distracted Montefort. The idea of going in to Clonmore deepened the pleasure of not yet stirring. Jane gave her longest yawn, at which Lilia, not without sombre pride, commented: "I don't wonder!" Leaning back, yawning also, fanning at her tea, she asked: "By the by, what did they have for dinner?"

Jane thought. "Well, we began with soup."

"Thick or clear? Clear, I should hope."

"It was semi-jelled. Then we had fish; I'm sure—yes, it was salmon."

"Well, go on."

Jane seemed to go off the air. She at last said: "Hash."

"Hash at that castle? No, it must have been salmi.— What did she wear?"

"Miles of chiffon," said Jane with gusto.

"What colour?"

"Yellow. The other woman wore black, tight."

"Men, then, were in the majority?"

"Yes.—We had pineapple water ice," the girl finished up with a rush. "The butler's name's Duffy, but he's going."

"And the chauffeur's?"

"I don't believe he told me."

Antonia wanted to know: "And your friend, what's *she* called?"

"Vesta," said Jane, defiantly.

"After a horse?"

"Well, so long as you did enjoy yourself," Lilia summed up. "I could not but wonder." She sighed and slowly put down her cup. "I ought not to ask you this, but did there appear to be at present anyone in her life?"

"Yes, Peregrine."

"What, a baronet?"

"Just a man."

"*I* see."

Lilia allowed her gaze to wander away towards the mountains. Her thoughts ranged also, leaving Jane and Antonia nowhere, in their trance of indifference. Under the tree the moist-green moss of the bench, the runnels worn in the stone, the small fern damply rooted into a crack spoke of the garden's lonely habituation to other weather—rain soughing through it and down the valley, or the drop-by-drop condensation of utter winter. But all now was clamped under a burning-glass. Today was a day for lizards—hazed colour shimmered, earth at a touch baked up through feet blunt in espadrilles. Kathie, having packed rhubarb into her apron, vanished —big leaves sprang back where she had stood.

"I say, Antonia!"

"Well, what?"

"Funny it sounds without the river." Antonia harkened, but said nothing. Jane went on in an other-worldly tone: "Quite soon, what will the cattle do?"

"What shall we have to be doing about the cattle?"

Lilia rolled her eyes their way. "Maud says the wireless says 'serious drought.' "

"Has Fred said anything?"

"Not that I know.—Maud needs another battery," Lilia was led to recall. She rose from the seat, shook out and smoothed her skirts. "If we are going we probably ought to go."

"Or why not," asked Antonia suddenly, "go to London?"

"Goodness gracious," the other said vaguely, vacantly, frowning at a tea-stain upon her bosom, "what ever are you talking about?"

"You.—How would you like to go to London?"

Lilia became appalled. "After all these years?" She looked for a second time at Antonia. "Are you feeling peculiar?"

"No, only thinking."

"What started you doing that?"

"You," reiterated Antonia.

"After all these years," Lilia said again, perspiring at the thought of them, bringing up her hankie to dab her face. "Go back to *there* again like a lost dog?"

"You need a change."

"I'm having my hair cut, aren't I?"

"Still," said Antonia fatefully, "think it over."

"So now you're bent on getting me out of here? What do you want, then—Fred all to yourself?"

"Oh, how can you be such a lunatic, Lilia, really!"

"Jane!" the mother called out, as loudly and wildly as though the girl were lost somewhere at the other end of the garden, "coming?" Off she painfully sped towards the distant sanctuary of the house; almost running, so that her toppling white heels were helplessly and perpetually turning over—sleeping-beauty briars along the choked path swung at her, clawing her Clonmore stockings. Her legs were at odds with each other—Lilia was slightly knock-kneed, as she had gracefully (it had been found, adorably) been as a young girl.

. . .

MAUD, sucking a clove ball, watched the street from the door of a Clonmore grocer, while inside her mother and sister shopped. The dark far end of Lonergan's was a bar, at which persons were drinking porter, and the interior smelled of that, along with sultanas, salted cod, brown sugar, biscuits, and green bacon. Jane, who for minutes had been side-tracked by a kitten in a crate of tomatoes, rejoined Lilia in time to see a couple of tins of Russian salad being added to what they had lately bought. She objected: "Oh, do we have to have that? Maud's going to say it is like vomit."

"In that case," declared Lilia, in a strong position, ready to tender a pound note, "she may leave the table."

"But it reminds *me* of something worse—delicatessens."

"They say it's not made in Russia."

"Delicatessens are in London."

"Then I can't see why; when you have such a happy life."

"Not eating things out of paper bags.—I wonder what Antonia meant just now?"

"Well, Jane, you heard her," Lilia pointed out.

This was the first occasion since leaving Montefort that the two of them had been out of Maud's hearing. While they hunted for salad-servers the child had trailed them; she compelled them to go with her to choose the battery; on the road in, she had kept a careful check on

her sister's management of the car. Lilia's morning outing, shopping with both her girls, had, thanks to
thoughtless, heartless words in the garden, all but gone
to pieces before the start: in the Ford, for instance, she
had sat mute while Jane first shaved a gatepost then
charged a bridge, so much was it one to her whether she
lived or died. Maud had gone with them to supervise
the making of the appointment at the hairdresser's for
an hour later—the establishment of that as a fixed point
did something to restore the day to stability. "You know
we'll be late for dinner," Maud had remarked, to which
her mother only returned: "That should give the rhubarb time to cool off." Clove balls had been bought to
allay Maud's hunger.

The two were now at a pause while semolina, which
Fred was believed to like, awaited its turn to be weighed
out. Jane, bracing her stomach against the counter, went
on: "I imagine she meant it kindly."

"You saw how upset I was."

"Antonia has sudden thoughts."

"She has deep-laid plans."

"I wonder . . ." pondered the girl, studying seed
cake under a clouded glass bell.

"*I* know," said her mother.

Jane raised the bell from the cake, let a fly out from
under, and put it down again. She said in a low voice:
"Weren't you engaged in London?"

"Engaged in what?"

"To Guy."

Lilia, dropping her voice lower than Jane's, to what could have sounded a furtive pitch, said: "We became engaged at Staines; that's not London."

All but accusingly Jane faced round, all eyes. "But you *were* there together. Fearfully happy—weren't you?"

Her mother replied with a dead smile. "That was the London of the past."

"But it must be that to somebody all the time."

Lilia appeared to count three before demanding: "And why should that make *you* scarlet in the face?"

"I didn't know I—"

" 'Guy,' indeed! He was older than your father."

"But not then."

"Quiet!—here comes the man!"

It was Mr. Lonergan, no less—till now detained at the other end of the shop, he came squeezing past his assistants behind the counter to accord at last to the ladies their meed of notice. Personally he brought them the semolina— "I hurried this on for you," he said. He balanced the bag down on the tins of salad, polished his right palm on his thigh, and shook hands with both of them. Lilia, who never grew used to this, made an inharmonious jab back at him with the pound note. She paid cash with dudgeon: seldom gone from her memory

was the unfortunate winter when Mr. Lonergan—owing, he later said, to some small kind of passing misun-
derstanding—had stopped the Montefort credit. She
would have transferred her custom but for the fact that
the whole of Clonmore would have known why. Upon
him, of course, nothing had left a ruffle: he was now
complimenting her on, by every sign, standing up very
well indeed to this wicked heat. He would go so far as
to say this was heathen weather, in which but for God
who was to predict what might happen next? They were
demented with it, he had heard, in England—as for
here, we were hardly to know ourselves. The advantage
of having the hay saved early was less when you looked
at cattle about to go mad with thirst—he hoped matters
were not that way at Montefort? Through it all, however, and come what might, concluded Mr. Lonergan—
taking in Jane, Lilia, and, in the doorway, Maud in the
act of kicking a dog which had been trying to lift its leg
—it was a great thing to be a united family. "The poor
little girl," he added. "Shall we see if there aren't any
sweeties for her?"

"No, thank you: that will be all today."

Mr. Lonergan's eyebrow did not go up; he said
gently: "More like a little present." Having briefed an
assistant, who unstoppered a jar, he filled a pause by
making a brushing gesture in the air over a cut ham.
"Flies get very bold," he remarked in a general way.

"My daughter's just let one out from over your cake."

"Ah, well, it would be a pity to let him suffocate." He seized the occasion to turn to Jane, as he had from the start been waiting to do. "Was it gay enough for you last night at the castle? I suppose you'd never know whom you'd find; still, they went to all lengths for you, sending the motor twice. And it makes for variety.—Had she the salmon?"

"Oh, yes."

"Jerry got it for her."

"Oh, poached, then?" flashed out the untutored girl. Mr. Lonergan looked at her austerely. "From time to time," he replied, "she gives custom locally.—So you sat down one under the number? Who was it, I wonder, never turned up?"

"I don't remember. It was a lovely party."

"They say her ladyship has great go." He deemed it right once more to address the mother. "Well, she's launched, it seems," he said, referring to Jane. "At this rate, who is to say that before we know we may not hear of her moving among the crowned heads?"

"There are practically none left," said Lilia stuffily.

"Thank you all the same, Mr. Lonergan," said the débutante, holding out her hand for the sweets for Maud.

"All that singsong about an immoral house," Lilia complained as they left the shop. "These people do noth-

ing but nose out money. And as I've always said to you,
spies everywhere. No, I never shall trust this country."

"You don't think that could be what Antonia—?"

"I've long ago given up thinking, thank you."

There on the curb outside Lonergan's, Lilia braced
her shoulders as though facing reality—looking up then
down the Clonmore straight wide main street at the
alternately dun and painted houses, cars parked askew,
straying ass-carts, and fallen bicycles. Dung baked on the
pavements since yesterday morning's fair; shop after
shop had insanely similar doorways, strung with boots
and kettles and stacked with calicoes—in eternal windows goods faded out. Many and sour were the pubs.
Overexposed, the town was shadeless—never a tree,
never an awning. Ice cream on sale, but never a café.
Clonmore not only provided no place to be, it provided
no reason to be, at all. So, but for the heat, was the place
at all times—but the glare today stripped it of even its
frowsty mystery, flattened it out, deadly glazed into a
picture postcard such as one might receive from Hell.
Gone was the third dimension; nothing stood behind
anything—opposite Lilia, a hillful of holy buildings appeared to weigh down the slated street roofs below. And
worst, wherever she turned her eyes movement could be
seen to expire slowly—a bus, it was true, came punting
in, but only to be at once deserted: why and how again
should it ever start? She could have pitied the bus. But,

like all else, it was absolute in its indifference to her.

"You know, Jane, this is a place where one could not even be run over."

"Well, it *was* nicer in the garden."

"Here I am, however."

"And while we are, do let's—"

"—You don't understand." Accumulated, the panic of twenty years broke in a wave over Lilia. "Where else, *now,* is there? For me, nowhere!"

"Oh, damn Antonia!" said Jane, really concerned. She relieved her mother of several parcels, dropped one or two of them, then said: "I'm sorry I mentioned Guy."

"As you say, the morning began so well.—And now, where for instance has Maud gone off to?"

"*I* thought, while we're waiting, let's have an ice?"

"I sometimes ask myself why I do wait for Maud."

"Oh, but I meant your hair appointment!"

Once more Lilia was rallied by that thought. "Well, I don't mind—but that there's no place I care to have ices in. Also, spoiling our dinners."

"Mother, one can't spoil rhubarb."

IF MISS FRANCIE'S *salon* possessed, alone in Clonmore, the art of reviving the life-illusion, one had only to know it to see why. It was up a flight of pink-linoed stairs. A breath of perfumed singeing emerged to meet one; triple net blinds shimmered over the outlook, and magazines, on a gilded wicker table, from time to time lavishly were renewed. Jane, her elbow sociably hitching back the curtain of the cubicle filled by Lilia, sat leafing through one of the magazines. Activity for the moment was at a stop—the sole drawback to Miss Francie was her elusiveness: heartwhole applications of zeal and charm were interspersed by mysterious total vanishings. *In medias res* she had a way of flitting right off her premises, leaving a lady clamped down under a drier, steaming into a towel, or half-shorn (which was Lilia's predicament). Nor did another step in to take her place, Miss Maeve, her reputed partner, being never not known to be either indisposed or away on holiday. The *salon* ran therefore behind schedule: happily, however, time did not press—who could wish to hurry to quit this magic oasis of tinted mirror, enamel, and Bakelite? And Miss Francie never failed to return in still better spirits for having been away. Her smiling non-explanations were somehow flattering, and her goings, though inconvenient, left not a wound.

Lilia, in a peach bib, half her hair on the floor, sat in a trance opposite her own reflection; which had become depersonalized by being so long regarded. So had that of her daughter, away behind her. No other clients were in the *salon*. She at length said: "Already I half *feel* different."

Jane raised her eyes, pronouncing: "Half of you looks different."

"You know my hair was once the colour of yours?"

"How nice," the girl said absently, kindly.

"Yes; I felt I took quite a step when I had it off."

"Once, it hung all the way down your back?"

"Yes—once."

"Do you remember yourself?"

"How do you mean?" asked Lilia, giving the bib a tug to loosen it slightly at the throat.

"Do you remember feeling lovely?"

"*Yours,* of course, was cut from the very start. But they still say a woman loses something."

"When was yours cut?"

"Shortly after the Armistice."

"By then, you did not care what you lost?"

"That was when bobbing came in, then shingling."

"Oh," accepted Jane. Her eyes drifted with polite slowness back to the magazine. Lilia slid her hand through the uncut side of her hair, comfortably savouring the discomfort. "I now do wonder how I so long endured this! . . . Jane?"

"Yes?"

"I wonder whatever's keeping her?"

"One could more imagine if one knew why she'd gone."

"You do sometimes talk like Antonia," Lilia remarked, though altogether idly, unacrimoniously. "You
could hardly not, I suppose, being so much with her."
She turned and reached out a hand for a magazine: "I
might just as well glance at one. Which have you got?"

"*Woman and Beauty.*"

"Give me a different one, then."

Jane supplied her with *Woman*. But after all, Lilia
did nothing more than contemplate, with her head
aslant, prototype Woman on the cover. Half back into
her trance, she remotely said: "I suppose they'll have had
the sense to begin dinner?"

"Father'll have to.—Your hair looks sad on the floor,
waiting just to be swept away!"

"Well, it's only litter, isn't it? Though I gave Guy a
piece once."

"A piece the colour of mine?"

"Then, it *was* something of myself! He wrapped it
round his finger into a ring, then laughed and slipped
it into his pocketbook. So I suppose it went back with
him to the Front."

"Aren't you certain?"

"Well, it must have. He never turned out that pocketbook; it was perpetually crammed with this and
that."

"What did he laugh at?"

"Laugh at when, do you mean?"

"When you said; when he ringed your hair round his finger."

"He regarded almost everything as a joke. I remember his train going out with them all singing. That train at the end of the last leave he ever had. What a dreadful station that was, full of nothing but draught and darkness and echoes—Charing Cross. He said: 'Why on earth did you come?' There's nothing so much in a goodbye, Jane—to my mind he seemed to be gone already. Some of those women went white as sheets; some of their faces gave me a shock—that was, after the train had gone. All *I* could do was stand and look at the clock; where to go next was what I could not imagine—he always had had some idea ready. The clock started me counting the hours back to how long ago it was since we'd both been dancing.—Did you know there once was a waltz called 'Destiny'?"

"I've danced to that!"

"But he and I *had* no destiny, in reality. No, none. I wonder why we had ever to meet at all."

"But you wouldn't have met Antonia, married Father, had me, if—"

"He and I, I said. What did it come to? Nothing."

"But you *had* that time!"

"And where is it all gone now? *He* knew, of course—

and so, how he did enjoy himself! My sister always said he was not serious."

"Mother, what *was* he like?"

"You keep on asking me, yet you think you know."

"Still, tell me!"

"I only knew what he was with me."

"What was he, with you?"

"Why, in love."

Jane got up, put down her magazine, and chose another—or rather, stood at the gilded table absently turning the others over. "I'm sure you're wrong," she asserted, "about having had no destiny. Couldn't it be a destiny to be someone something had once happened to?"

"But more has happened to me than that."

"Oh—has there?"

"For one thing, there was your father."

A FACT unknown to Jane was that, some seven years after her first child's birth, Lilia had made a bolt for London. Whether Montefort or Fred's taciturnities or his infidelities, actual or supposed, all of a sudden became too much for her never went on to record: she simply wrote that she was not expecting to be returning. The letter reached Fred at the height of harvest: he had

had no time to do more than post it on to Antonia, with
a marginal scribble in his own hand—he indeed, he
said, felt badly if this was his fault. Young Jane was being, he added, as good as gold. Antonia, given to picture
what a high time must have set in at Montefort, had
been as much riled by Fred's equanimity as by his wife's
defection. She had cut short a tour abroad and gone
straight to Fulham, where, in the maisonette of her
sister (then still living) Lilia inevitably was. Some time
went to breaking the truant down. Repetitions of "I will
never go back to him!" at the start almost passionate, had
grown fainter. Where, in that case, *did* Lilia intend to
go? That had produced a blank though obstinate silence.

"And what," Antonia pursued, "do you plan to live
on?—Your sister?"

Lips had been compressed. "No: I have money."

"That's impossible!"

"Yes; I have parted with my engagement ring."

"You don't mean Guy's?"

"Yes I do," had maintained the poor mouth. "What
else had I? Fred never gave me one."

"Damn: I forgot to see to that!—Still, he needs you."

"He's got Jane."

"Yes—and who's to look after *her?*"

"*That's* why you expect me to go back?"

"Fred wants you back."

"Who says so? Never a line from him."

"He's got his pride and he hasn't got your address. Idiot, *because* he needs you he's got his pride!"

"He can look for someone to do the chickens."

"Obviously, he loves you—if you must have it!"

"How many years, I wonder, is it since he gave me a sign of that?"

"He's a queer fish, remember."

"What do *you* know of Fred?"

Antonia's letter to Fred had opened by asking about the harvest: "This year, how have we done?" She hoped, not too badly—for she must now request him to turn his attention to something else. *In re* Lilia, what had he thought of doing? In her own view, there were not two ways about it—it was up to him to come over and patch things up. The sooner the better. Lilia would *come* back but never *go* back—let Fred use his head and see the distinction! She gave the Fulham address and enclosed a cheque—for, she said, incidental expenses. For a week, she said, she would ask no questions: by the end of that week she would expect to hear of their both being back, as before, at Montefort. For, she need not remind him, the taking-on (and that meant permanent taking-on) of Lilia had been his side of the bargain. Or was he proposing to let the whole thing lapse? If so, she must make other plans for Montefort—sorry as she would be. And womanless, of course, he could not keep

Jane: sad, but, as he no doubt saw, the child would have
to be handed over.—If he cared to know, Lilia was most
unhappy. Speechless, helpless. Other than Fred, whom
had she?

Fred's reaction to Antonia's whip-cracking had been
forthwith to tear up the cheque. He was about to tear up
the letter too, but scowled and meditated again over the
threat in its final sentences. Paris was worth a Mass: he
did in the end go to London, and re-wooed Lilia. The
reconciliation, although brief, was signalized by the con-
ception of Maud. Antonia succeeded in tracing, and
bought back, the hoop of sapphires chosen by Guy for
Lilia: she posted the ring to its owner at Montefort—
the packet arrived when Lilia was in the throes of morning sickness. Nothing was spoken of again.

Maud put the lid on everything. . . . Jane, however,
just could recall the homecoming; Lilia fresh from
London, languidly-dashingly new in a scarlet suit, dropping a kiss on the head of her harmless daughter, and in
the same way bestowing a florid doll on the child who
marvelled: "She does not mind me." "She could afford
to love me, or almost thought so," Jane could have almost thought. The memory, apart from containing
scarlet, was the more brilliant for having no shadow of
sense—could she have dreamed it? was it out of a novel?
Nothing before or after gave it support. Among other
scenes, the picture fitted in nowhere; it was like a card

astray from another pack. There it somewhere was, but it did not trouble the girl. Moreover Jane, it must be recalled, had till now never courted memories—all her own had been random; the awesome attraction of other people's had not been felt by her till now.

"OH, OF course," Jane said civilly, "there was Father."

"There still is."

"Yes," agreed the girl, more uneasily, "yes, of course. But one forgets people when they are always there." She bent over the magazine, falling silent, till her mother remarked: "*That* almost sounds like her coming back. Whoever is she talking to on the stairs?"

Miss Francie re-entered, with a reminiscent smile. She glided towards and picked up the pink comb, flourished it, and set upon Lilia's hair as though fresh inspiration had come in absence. Lilia quivered— "You'll get both sides the same?"

"If we don't," vowed Miss Francie gaily, "we'll do still better!—Your little girlie's waiting, down on the stairs: I all but fell over her. Aren't children wonderfully patient!"

"What was Maud doing?"

"Whatever it was, she was deep in it. Tell me now, has she ever some kind of a dream companion?"

VIII

THE intensity of a brought-about recollection leaves one worn down; it consumes cells of the being if not the body. Truth goes on to eat through the weakened fabric. That afternoon, when the others had gone to sleep and Fred off into his working limbo, Lilia returned to the stone bench, in search of the serenity left behind there. But not a trace of the morning was in the garden—the tanglewood had closed in again on its own story; aloof stood the sundial; only the parching colours lingered mockingly on. To be less alone, she had come out carrying sewing—she was at work on a pink chemise. But dipping in vain for scissors into her workbox, grimacing as she bit off threads, she still stood under that station clock. The clock-hands stood still: she was seventeen.

The mistake had been, going to see Guy go—that altogether had been too lifelike. Saying to Jane "he was gone already," she had put the feel of the thing at its least awful. What obstinacy, what cry of her growing heart for even this as a consummation had, in spite of

all, brought her to that last train? For the fact was, he
had told her not to be there. Yet there, with a trembling
conventionality, Lilia was. Khaki, khaki—over the
crowds she finally, victorious, saw his head turning this
way, that way, searching for something, someone. She
swam with her elbows, got through, touched him.
Round flashed his face, lit up—only to fall. "Why on
earth did *you* come?" She told him: "I wanted to see the
last of you," and, pulling her glove off, made him see, as
one might show a pass, the engagement ring's day-or-
night-blue winking sapphires. "Yes," he agreed, "do
wear it! You'll wear it, won't you?"

"Always."

So he had kissed her. Tied in a flapper bow, her hair
meanwhile swung down to her waist: reaching round
her, he tweaked at a tip of it, and his arm was with her a
moment longer. So they stood, re-enacting what was all
done with. "Be a good girl," he told her, tenderly, last-
ingly, lightly, "and go home—won't you?" She broke
away, wanting only to vanish. But she found herself
walled in, wedged to a stop amongst rooted oblivious
sayers of the goodbye. Hardly more than three steps was
she from where he was, with no shelter from him but her
turned-away back. Somebody then heaved in between
him and her. She had no means of not overhearing him
exclaim: "*You!*"

The "*You!*" came out of him in tone unknown, unfamiliar to Lilia, familiar elsewhere. Memorably a voice came back with: *"Why not, after all? I'm the family."* . . . *"Why, for God's sake, then, didn't you wear a hat?"* . . . *"I've no idea. What an inferno! Where's this girl you're marrying?"* . . . *"Been and gone."* . . . *"Then who were you looking out for?"* . . . *"Just a face."* . . . *"Oh, a face, yes?"* . . . *"A face I might possibly see again."* . . . *"How possibly?"* . . . *"You never know, you know."* . . . *"Well, I'll be moving on."* . . . *"No, stop a minute."* . . . *"No, I think I'll be moving on."* . . . *"No, stop a minute; listen, Antonia."* . . . *"These infernal echoes."* . . . *"All right, go, then!"*

He added: *"You'll never see the last of me!"*

Antonia, unlike Lilia, got clean away—so fast that the fiancée, though craning her neck, never so much as set eyes upon the cousin, though one could keep track of her thrusting course. Lilia indeed effected her own escape in the backwash from the fleeing Antonia, and so got to safety under the clock. There she stayed, ascribing thoughts to herself, putting on again the glove she had taken off—that done, being able to think of no other kind of livingness to imitate, she seceded from life and became marble. She set up as a statue, posed there smirking at nothing—and why not? Nothing made sense, till at last it seemed the station had heard the train with him in it, gone, go—cheers were no more, nor was the singing. Blindly those who began to weep streamed past. Nothing was left behind but the overheard words.

It was not to be thought of, so never was. *Had* it been seen again, that awaited face? *Had* she come to the train, that last-moment comer? If so, who was she; if not, what was she not? *Was* she—did she exist? Did he expect her, did he invent her? There had stood he and Antonia, jibing at one another up to the end. "You never know, you know." Better uncertainty; best no answer. Who desires to know what they need not? So why continue to wonder, so why suffer? Yes, but if not the Beloved, what was Lilia? Nothing. Nothing was left to be.

And now these letters. To whom, why?

Are you to be leaving me nothing, O Guy, then?

Lilia let fall her sewing. A pink-silk reel ran from her along the bench, to be stopped in the crack where the fern grew. A young thrush flew in affright from the twisted apple tree, and away in a corner a door creaked: somebody had come in and was in this garden. But not again a sound, not a step—there ensued more than a silence of moss, sloth, airlessness, and the exhausted river: something more than human was at intensity. In depth, dead-still, branches screened the doorway—of whom was this the ghost in the afternoon?

Only since Guy's day was it that undeniably the roses had run to briar, the wall so loosened as to start falling

stone by stone down into the ravine. Now it was not so
much that decay was more rapid or widespread, but that
it was apparent—out it stood! Nothing now against it
maintained the place. Struggle there was, as not in his
day; but never a heedless victory—gone was the master-
touch of levity, nerve, or infatuation. The crazed perfection he saw, once, into the place left a trace of itself,
but in such a way as to make it the more to be felt to be
gone, with him. Yes, in his way he had kept Montefort
up—up, that was, to his own high idea of it. Hard was it
not to tax him with, by having carelessly turned away,
having somehow hastened the trend to ruin in such life
or lives as his own had touched. By striking when it did,
before he had tried to see, even, whether he *could* con-
solidate, death made him seem a defaulter, a runner-out
upon his unconsummated loves. He had stirred up too
much; he had scattered round him more promises as to
some dreamed-of extreme of being than one man could
have hoped to live to honour. Yet, on the other hand,
had he come back, had he lived out the ordinary day,
would this extraordinary power of his illusion have
stayed so strongly? As it was, here it hung in the air over
scene and people, going on affecting them, working on
them, causing them most to dread to decline from being
as once he saw them, and most to desire they knew not
what. He had not finished with them, nor they with
themselves, nor they with each other: not memories was

it but expectations which haunted Montefort. His immortality was in their longings, while each year more
mocked the vanishing garden.

Lilia supposed only one thing—"You've come to tell
me?" Her heart beat wonderfully calmly: she retrieved
the pink reel, pressed it into her workbox, closed the lid,
laid her folded sewing upon it, and sat to wait. She took
a view of her left hand, now only dressed in Fred's wedding ring, while hop by hop nearer came back the
thrush, unbelievingly fixing her with its eye. Amazement surrounded her but was not her own; second after
second was to be counted by the apprehensive springing
and landing of the bird, whose prints left here and there
a smudge in the dust. No longer could she abide the
waiting to know: suddenly she stood up and, bringing
her workbox with her, perhaps to show him how deedy
her married days were, set off down the path which led
to the door, proceeding or wading through the white
glare with the majesty or immunity of a sleepwalker.
Not an enemy briar dared cross her way now Lilia was
not retreating but advancing.

But just short of the corner of the path, she already—
as one does see the brilliant image of him or her whom
one is to meet in reality in a moment—saw him. Both
were deep in love. The breathless girl stopped to put
down the woman's workbox under a bush, then, head
higher than ever, went round the corner.

Virginia creeper camouflaged the wall round the door, an over-painted showering of bronze-green. Leaves and tendrils, caught as they always were by the pushing-inward opening of the door, draped themselves over the orifice in fringes. The door *was* open—as to everything else the creeper demented and drowned sight by giving it no one point to rest on. The Guy who had come in her eye with her round the corner was transfixed first here, then there, then nowhere against the creeper—facelike seemings of faces, but never his, were everywhere on the chequer of light-and-shade. Not yet, not yet was there quite no one—to be gone, a man must have been here! The tearing-out of the centre of the picture still left a quiver of edges torn—she stood in a stupor, some way away down the path. Then Fred came back again through the door: he stared and said: "You *are* there, then, after all?"

"Why?"

"I was looking for you."

She marvelled: "In the middle of the afternoon?" laughed, and gave a running totter towards him. He met the totter, catching her by the elbows—"Steady," he enjoined, as to Jane last night. "Look, what's the matter? You're as white as a ghost. Why sit in a sun like today," he wanted to know, "when you've just had your hair off?"

"You noticed, then?"

"Antonia said that was why you were in Clonmore. But I should have."

Upheld by him by the elbows, having the sensation that her feet were being washed away from under, but that she did not need them, Lilia, from nearer to it than she had been to it for years, studied Fred's chest, numbering the buttons gone from the shirt. She ventured: "Why?"

"It somehow makes you look younger—or anyway you looked different when I saw you."

"Saw me?"

"When I came through the door."

"I saw Guy, I thought."

He gave her a shake and said: "Then you have got sunstroke! Come on, come in."

She groped for the ground with her feet and began to walk; they went through the door, which Fred pulled to with a creak behind them, and along the passage into the yard—Kathie, carrying buckets, passed them. Down on to them fell the blistered shadow of the deserted buildings; up rose Montefort's unsightly and streaked backview, shutters half-folded, whitish, over the windows of unused rooms. Lilia, by lagging mutely on Fred's arm, indicated she either did not wish to go in or was not ready to go in yet, so he went on steering their course haphazardly, out across the yard to the carriage archway. All at once she showed will: "We'll sit on that." "That" being the mounting-block, they did so; she on the top, he on a step. As she knew, they had never in all their story (if indeed story it could be called) together stopped in the dense green gloom under this particular chestnut tree.

"Good," he said, relieved, "—that is, if you're all right?" Though for his part he hardly knew what to do with the immobility.

She asked him: "Now—what did you want?"

"I'm not so sure this is quite the moment."

"Why not, Fred? I mean, after all?"

"But I mean, after just now. It might only upset you over again."

"*I* was not upset," she said with a little laugh.

"Well, I wish I knew," he confessed—to himself, not her. Sitting where he sat, he stretched one leg out, heaved a little over, began to tug something bulky out of a pocket. By the time she looked to see what was happening, the wadge of letters was in his hands, cross-tied with a white satin ribbon, probably Jane's. "My one idea," he said, "was to get these back to you." But as things now were he stayed frowning, weighing them in his hands.

She recoiled. "You don't mean *those* are the ones?"

"You ought to know. Aren't they?"

"Who says so?" she asked, in a voice of still greater fear.

"Maud. Offered them to me for ten bob."

"No, I don't believe you!"

"Yes, tracked 'em down to wherever Jane had been keeping them."

"And you gave her all that money?"

"Me? I shook the hell out of her—and that's *my* kid, the dirty little so-and-so!"

She by habit said: "It's more that she's mercenary. . . . Nor were they Jane's, if it comes to that."

He burst out: "Anyway, here they are, so for God's sake take them!" He thrust them her way, looking neither at them nor her. "D'you suppose *I* want to carry them round?"

She hung back. "*You* know they're mine, from him, then?"

"Who'm I to know—how should I know?—Why, aren't they?"

That caused her to snatch at them, as though they, impatiently tendered, might after all at the next instant be withdrawn. Having them, she went on to hold them numbly, viewing the writing quartered by white ribbon with a distant, suspended fascinated mistrust. "Well, he wrote them, all right," she at last gave out.

"Remember them, then, do you?"

"I—I don't know, yet."

"Then look again, why not? You can read, can't you? Go on, untie them!"

"Fred," she pleaded.

"Well?"

"Why ever didn't you burn them?"

He was astounded—either at being asked or, more likely, because he had not thought of it. It was to be doubted if he had thought at all; he had acted, and with precipitation. For the brainstorm set up in him by Maud's overture, for his inordinate violence to the child (whom actually he had not only shaken but struck, battered at, in wrenching the letters from her), there was no reason he cared or dared to fathom. Though the worst had subsided, passion was still racing through his system—had not Lilia unerringly thrown herself on his breast? No, he had not thought because he had never stopped to; his course had forced itself on him, which made it still seem right—or if not quite right, right enough: there had not been choice. In an outsize issue, what man ever decides? One is decided for. *Now*, however, she asked him . . . To gain time he brought out a cigarette, struck a match, but did not at once light up— instead, he contemplated the orange flame, brought into being by him like a soul by God, but unlike a soul in being without a tremor in the stillness of the drought. In-and-out under the archway, the Ford's old tracks crisscrossed in mud set hard like cement.

"You set store by them, didn't you?" he asked finally.

"No, but I never wanted them," she cried out, though

restlessly testing at the ribbon. "How could I ever bear to read them again; even if I did ever read them before? No, you're only driving me mad, Fred, waiting to watch me! What d'you want to know—whether they *are* to me? How am *I* to know after all these years, or indeed care? Yes, I said 'care,' Fred. From what Jane gives out, these are love letters—well, what if they are? What's it all about? What he's saying here well might not make sense to me any longer, whether it *was* to me or to who knows who else. No, Fred, thanks: give them back to Jane."

"O.K., then," Fred said. "Then I needn't have worried."

She at once glanced downward at the top of his head. "Though that's not to say," she added, "in spite of all, that I've so altogether forgotten what love was."

He gave one of his yawns, mechanically heaved himself off the step, stood clear of the mounting-block, stretched all over. "Ought to be going." From where she sat on the top, Lilia's legs hung crossed at the ankles, heels eased clear of her shoes: one of the dangling white shoes now fell off, whereupon he strolled round and picked it up for her. Soiled, it had once been pretty; and as it was it partly fretted and partly humoured him. "Come on, then, give it here," he suggested, meaning for her to stretch the foot out to have the shoe put back on again, which was done. "But you still have to go?" she said.

"I said I ought to; and so I ought." He let his cigarette drop and stamped it out, as one might the temptation to linger, but none the less went on to study his wife, one could not be certain how retrospectively. In the taut blue lap of her frock remained the letters; he whistled a bar, then asked: "What made you say you saw him?"

"Thought I did."

"But what made you tell me?"

She turned her eyes upon him. "What makes you ask?"

"I naturally wondered." He was looking away, at a crack high up near where the keystone was, in the facial stucco of the archway: about to whistle a bar more, he seemed to stop to debate whether he should.

"You took me," she told him, "quite by surprise."

"You made *me* jump, I don't mind telling you—standing there! I hardly believed my eyes."

"Neither could I."

"Hardly knew who I was?"

She first lowered, then shook her head: "I saw *you*. That was the shock."

He jibed: "What, never saw me before?"

"Go on—laugh!"

"No; you just had a touch of the sun." He looked behind at the exposed nape of her neck, then clapped a hand on his own, instructively—"There's where it gets you, there, if you don't watch out."

Lilia said: "All I know is, someone *was* in that garden, and for a reason known to me. How am I to tell you for how long; well do I remember how it felt—each knowing the other to be there. And there was more to it than that, Fred. What was about to take place I shall often wonder—all I did was stop sewing and watch the bird watch me. You know *I* was never one to imagine; and how was I to imagine it could be you? As we now are, anything seemed more likely. Guy seemed more likely, dead as he is."

"What d'you mean," he said, " 'as we now are'?"

"You know you know. What's the use of asking?"

He gave a frown.

She put her hands to her face and added: "As we have come to be."

He came and stood closer by where she sat, leaning, putting pressure against her shoulder. "All the same," he said, "I was looking for you."

"You didn't look far. There I was, only there on that seat."

"Must be years since I've been into that garden. It's all gone to seed, or something—gives me the creeps."

"We used to go in there when we first got married."

"That creeper's getting to choke the door."

"Well, all you had to do was to give a shout."

"You make me laugh," he declared. "Shout, for you? And what would I get for that?—'What is it now, Fred?

. . . Oh, my poor head: can I never be left in peace!
. . . Why can't you ever leave me alone?'—That's how
you go on," he said, bending a sideways look at her.

"Well, I never know, Fred."

"What don't you know?"

"It's more that I know too well. You mean all right;
you intend to be good to me. But it's always that, and
that's what gets on my nerves."

"Yes, I get on your nerves, all right. I feel sorry for
you."

She drew away from his shoulder. Pick, pick, pluck,
her fingers went at the ribbon bow on the letters, till,
furious, she swept the packet aside, to burst out: "Oh,
Fred, what a thing to say!"

"I don't see why. It must be tough to have nerves,
apart from having anyone on them. You've had bad luck
all along, and I'm part of it. You had a bad come-down,
after all you'd been, in the first place, led on to expect
and hope for. You never should have had to put up with
me, but there it was: that was how things worked out.
There we were, and in consequence here we are. When I
feel you don't make the best of a bad job, I always try
to consider how bad the job is—that's to say, from your
point of view. Nothing much to take your mind off anything, is there? Stuck here, I mean, with the money short
and most of the time no one, all these long winters. Year
in, year out."

"There's year in, year out been you."

"That's been the trouble."

"Why, do you think, Fred? *Are* we so unsuited?"

"Well, I don't know," he pondered. "*I* should not have said so—that is, at one time. We made out all right, once, in our own way. You know when that was."

"Yes," she said. Again a shoe fell off, this time to be left to lie on the ground.

"I've never quite understood," he went on. "Maybe there could have been something more for us, that we missed; if so, I probably bungled things. Nothing came out of our making love, and I'd no way to show you anything more. I was never Guy."

"I did not expect you to be."

"That was just it. For my not being what he was, you had it in on me."

"You said we'd been once happy."

"We made out, till the thing started galling me."

"If you'd only . . ."

"Oh, well, why talk?" he asked.

"With that idea in your head, what was I to do?"

"What you did do—barely put up with me."

"You went off."

"And if I did? I go where I'm wanted."

"Still, Fred?"

He shrugged his shoulders.

She said: "You never gave me a chance."

"Well, I don't know, Lilia. I took a chance on you."

"No, Antonia made you."

"Still, I still took a chance. Thought there ought to be something in Guy's girl."

In answer she drew up her body, trembling. She pressed her palms over her eyes. The air between them may have recorded something, for he turned, saying: "Don't take it that way. Am I saying there wasn't? But not for me, never for me—now was there?"

"Wasn't there ever, Fred?"

"Are you asking me?"

From under her hands she said: "You are the one who ought to know."

The chestnut, darkening into summer, canopied them over; over their heads were its expired candles of blossom, brown—desiccated stamen were in the dust. Over everything under the tree lay the dusk of nature. Only the car-tracks spoke of ever again going or coming; all else had part in the majestic pause, into which words were petering out. This was not so much a solution as a dissolution, a thinning-away of the accumulated hardness of many seasons, estrangement, dulledness, shame at the waste and loss. A little redemption, even only a little, of loss was felt. The alteration in feeling, during the minutes in which the two had been here, was an event, though followed by a deep vagueness as to what they should in consequence do or say. Impossible is it for persons to be changed when the days they have still to live stay so much the same—as for these two, what could be their hope but survival? Survival seemed more possible now, for having spoken to one another had been an act of love. No word, look, or touch was for some time to be needed to add more: instinctively now they rested, almost apart, under the saturating chestnut, with what they knew at work in them slowly. Only kept from slipping from Lilia's lap by the idle hold of one of her hands, the letters were neither more nor less part of the scene than the spent match or the dropped shoe.

Light long footsteps, though not harkened to, were none the less to be heard in the stable yard. Jane stopped, however, short in the archway. She stared at those two beings whom, with a start, she perceived to be her father and mother.

IX

MAUD, limping a little, paced to and fro under the Montefort front windows, outside the lowly front-garden fence. An open prayer-book was in her hands. Her movement had the monotony of a pendulum's; her voice, loudly rising and falling, only came to a pause when, from time to time, she leafed ahead through the Psalms for more maledictions.

"They compassed me about also," she was now intoning, *"with words of hatred, and fought against me without a cause.*

"For the love that I had unto them, lo, they take my contrary part; but I give myself unto prayer.

"They have rewarded me evil for good, and hatred for my goodwill.

"Set Thou an ungodly man to be ruler over him, and let Satan stand at his right hand. When sentence is given upon him, let him be condemned, and let his prayer be turned into sin.

"Let his days be few, and let another take his office.

"*Let his children be fatherless, and his wife a widow.*

"*Let his children be vagabonds, and beg their bread;
let them seek it also out of desolate places.*

"*Let the extortioner consume all that he hath, and let
the stranger spoil his labour.*

"*Let there be no man to pity him, nor to—*"

"*Stop* it, Maud!" shouted a voice within. A moment
later, rending curtains apart, Antonia appeared at her
bedroom window. "Stop it, I say."

"I have," said the child, looking sternly up.

"Or go," said the other, weakening, "and play somewhere else."

"I am not playing."

"What d'you think you're doing?"

"Calling down vengeance. Couldn't you hear me?"

Antonia was at a disadvantage. Her whole voice had
spent itself on the shout; behind her dark-glaring glasses
her eyes felt gummy. Pitchforked back again into the
abnormalities of the afternoon, her spirit shrank from
it all within her, without capacity, unfresh as the clothes
in which she had slept. The beheld landscape, woods
edging the gorge, cattle dotting the rise to the obelisk,
seemed not so much unreal as real at her own expense.
Apart from the manner of being wakened, it was un-
pleasing to be again awake. And to cap all, one was con-
fronting Maud—who herself wore, though never with
more composure, a select air of having been through

hell. "Why do *you* look so bunged-up?" Antonia asked reluctantly.

"Could I speak to you, Cousin Antonia?"

"You are, aren't you?"

Maud glanced at the cattle and said: "Alone."

"Why?"

"Because of something."

"Can't you find someone else?"

"It depends who. Father has assaulted me."

Antonia, digging for wax in one ear, said somewhat unfavourably: "Rats. Why should he?"

"May I come up?"

"No," said Antonia, preparing to quit the window. "Tell it to the Marines. I don't feel well."

Maud looked still more sombre. "Then I ought to tell Mother."

"Heavens, and raise the roof?—though you're clearly mad, Maud. All right, all right, all right then: come on up.—But for a minute, mind!" Antonia groaned and went to cold-sponge her face; she thought of a drink, but up here was none.

Maud selected a blade of grass, placed it in as a marker, and closed her prayer-book. She was to be heard to progress upstairs. She dealt three taps to Antonia's door.

Antonia, from the washstand, said: "*Now*—what is it?" The child entered this room unknown to her with

an inhuman absence of awe or interest. She took her
bearings, but in an abstract way—the draped dishevelled
big bed, prodigal dressing-table, strewn sofa, and cav-
ernous open wardrobe were to her eye no more than
what they in fact were, furniture. Here where Lilia had
lingered to raise scenes, there where Jane so often gracefully had disposed herself fell Maud's glance—noting,
neutral, impervious. She was a little bothered by the
unforeseeingness of the various chairs, of which no one
seemed to have got itself into what could be considered
a key position. The room represented an opportunity—
apart from that, being allowed in here so clearly meant
little to her that one saw how little it had meant to be
kept out. She sat down, though always with the air of
expecting she might do better later.

Antonia, wringing at the sponge, demanded: "Just
what did happen?"

"He knocked me about."

"Where?"

"All over."

"No, I mean where did this happen?"

"Near the gate of the Horse Field."

"What were you doing?"

"Nothing. He twisted my arm. He swore."

"Good heavens."

"He gnashed his teeth. He even trod on my toe."

Antonia, measuring out mouthwash, remarked: "Yes,

he saw red, apparently. Come on, Maud—what *had* you been doing to him?"

"Just standing there."

"Well, you must ache all over. But I can't see where we others come into this."

"He seized your letters, Cousin Antonia."

Antonia, blank, asked: "What on earth do you mean?"

"Those ones there is being this fuss about."

"Stop, though—who said they were mine?"

"Everything in this house belongs to you."

Antonia stood and swilled round her mouth, then gargled.

"Mother always says so," averred Maud.

"I daresay," said Antonia, having done. "But in any case, what were *you* doing with them?"

"They were under a stone under a tree."

"I daresay: till you came along and pinched them. Having, of course, no notion who'd put them there?"

"Jane. But they were not hers."

"Who are you to say so?"

"You said so, yesterday. At dinner."

Spat-out mouthwash reddened Antonia's basin. She stonily went on to look to see, in the glass above, what first sleep then water out of the jug had succeeded in doing to her make-up. "Cold cream!" she commanded, hand out, forgetting Maud was not Jane. Maud justifiably did not budge. "Oh, all right," grunted Antonia, "I'll get it." But she gave up the idea; seating herself, instead, on her bed at the pillow end, back up against the damask panel. "Jane set store by those letters," she said judicially, "wrongly or rightly. Didn't you know?"

"Yes. That was why I knew they should go to Father."

"Now, why on earth?"

"Because he *is* our Father.—Or was," Maud added, after a dreadful pause, testing the reflex in a wrenched shoulder.

"So you—? But you told me just now he seized them."

"The sight of them threw him into that fury."

Antonia refolded her arms. "You were holding out on him, eh? What for, eh—fun?"

"How could it have been fun, Cousin Antonia?" the child asked, not so much scornfully as thoughtfully, gimleting through her inquisitor with her eyes.

"Money, then?" supplemented the other quickly.

Maud looked away, though only to think again. "He once promised I was to have ten shillings."

"Why?"

"For not pestering Mother, if I had not. And I haven't."

"As you took the chance to remind him?—But look here, though, Maud, if you needed cash why didn't it strike you to come to me? *I* could have been interested in those letters."

Maud blinked, for the first time. "But they're yours anyhow."

"Would that stop me from wanting to have them back? For all you know, I might have been good for a pound."

"Father needed them more, Cousin Antonia."

"What on earth made you think that? Whatever for?"

"To put a stop to their being around."

"You really think that?"

"Yes. It made him look small."

"What did?"

"Those letters being around."

"But they weren't," said Antonia. "Jane had them."

With contempt Maud said: "They went on being around."

"What's your father done with them?"

"I don't know. I fell down and he walked away. I bled."

"Well, another time leave things where you find them. Or don't find them."

"*You* know who found them, Cousin Antonia. I only afterwards saw where they'd been put." The child looked towards the washstand. "May I wash the blood off my frock?"

"No; not in here," said Antonia sharply. "You've probably simply been tearing at your hives."

"No, I fell on my knee. And I could be bleeding internally."

"Not you, Maud."

"Mother's known that to happen."

"Well, look how you knock other people about."

This was true. Maud was specially feared by children with whom she attended school. Complaints from parents filtered through to Montefort; rumour enlarged upon her doings. Rare were school days unmarked by instances of aggression; studious classroom and play-hour yard alike offered her outlets, but it was the transport provided for the Protestant children which on the whole best lent itself to her purpose. A motor vehicle known in the locality as the Protestant Van circulated around these roads twice daily, gleaning up or delivering home again outlying pupils; and low sank, each school-day morning, the hearts of those already pent up within as a slowing-down announced the approach to Montefort. Maud, in wet weather rendered still more terrible by a pixie hood, and often perched atop of a cracked gatepost, was to be found contemplatively waiting, one knew for what. The Protestant Van—it had been said—became like a bag of cats inside from the moment Maud stepped up into it. For she knew not only how to begin but how to beget fights. Terminate as they might in hobnailed boots, still were the shins of

young boys exposed and tender; the no less blameless
tweetering little girls pinkly invited pin-sticking, hair-
pulling, pinching. Retaliation at least attempted caused
Maud from time to time to be black-and-blue, or proudly
scarred in the face like a student dueller. But somehow
the little Protestants in the van never effectively did
combine against her—so did she sow dissension in their
ranks that when deposited at the school entrance they
were in a state of all-round bad blood and suppurating
mutual suspicion. A point to be noted about Maud was
that she confined her attacks to her co-religionists: she
had never been heard of kicking a Catholic child.

It also was true, now, that though Maud thought fit
to play up her bodily injuries, no great complaint as to
them was really suggested: she *was* injured, but in some
other way. Antonia's reference to her prowess caused
her only just to restrain herself from an impersonal,
non-disclaiming smile—the idea could have been pleas-
urable enough, but just now was unhappily not the time
for it. She so redisposed the hem of her skimpy frock
as to lay bare the slightly blood-clotted knee—not so
much, it seemed, for Antonia's benefit as her own; for,
heels hitched up under her on the chair-rung, she bent
forward as though actually communing with the wound.

Antonia said: "And leave him alone, in future."

"I shall not need to. God will have cast him out."

"*Maud,* don't be so pompous and blasphemous!"

"He's cast himself out of *my* sight," the child inexorably went on. "This has shown what he is. I have done my best; I have never not treated him as my Father. I did my duty to him, and now you see. I've done all in my power to set him up as ruler over his own house, even when it's been your house, Cousin Antonia. His word ought to have been law, so I have very often obeyed him. If I'm to have a Father, I don't choose to have a Father who's not thought of highly, at any rate by me. I've been to a lot of trouble, honouring him. But in spite of all, there he went about, this last day or two, looking small. Why should I put up with that?"

"Nonsense; he's not a small man—nothing makes him look it."

"He's looked like nothing," the pitiless Maud pronounced.

Antonia marvelled: "How you do come to conclusions!"

"Yes, Cousin Antonia, I do."

"*And* act on them—really one could admire you!"

"Father did not," Maud said, with curling lip.

"He didn't know, I expect, as well as you and I do, what you were up to."

"What do you know I was up to?" asked the child, showing, for the second time in this interview, a flicker of speculation as to Antonia.

"A purge, perhaps?"

"I don't know what's come over this place," Maud stated. "However, the Lord did, so in despair He showed me what I had better do."

"And did the Lord suggest your sticking up your father for ten shillings?"

"No, I thought of that," said Maud, not turning a hair.

"Your motives were a bit mixed, didn't it strike you?"

"I'd been to a good deal of trouble, Cousin Antonia."

"Spying on Jane? Yes, I suppose you had. Well, I can only say what I said before—you might have found *me* good for a pound!"

"I daresay," agreed Maud, in a voice for the moment abstracted, for she was rubbing spittle, on the remote chance of its still being possible to avert blood-poisoning, into the rawer parts of her grazed knee. "But I was considering what was right or wrong. It was merely that I also needed ten shillings."

"If it comes to that, they *were,* as you say, my letters."

Maud stretched her frock till it once more covered her knee, then pointed out: "They were Father's thorn in the flesh."

"And were altogether doing no good, you thought?"

"That's for you to say, Cousin Antonia. You were the one who knew Cousin Guy."

"So it's generally thought, Maud. Generally thought."

Tilting her head back against the bed-head, Antonia closed her eyes, having for far too long had a view of this room and all in it, including Maud.

The nature of the outrage this afternoon became clear enough—rather clearer, perhaps, than one wished it to. To invite or allow any more from Maud would be to get in irretrievably deep with the Old Testament. Antonia, so many of whose days here, or indeed in these days almost anywhere, went by in a haze of suspended notice, was struck, and the more because so suddenly, by the obstinacy and, to give her her due, patience with which Maud had gone on giving Fred a build-up. The child's requiring life to be patriarchal was not, now that one thought of it, so surprising; but one never had thought of it—why should one? Maud and Fred, indeed, were the last two persons one in any way connected with one another. Maud as a character had to be re-assessed—she was a bandit not out of contempt for law but out of contempt for its missingness from Montefort: she in fact was the purest authoritarian. She had put into power, one might say forced into being, a father-figure: this had collapsed on top of her in the Horse Field. Wrath need not necessarily have ill become Fred; if anything, anger became a father. But he had made an exhibition of himself—the last thing she ever wanted to see. He had been human, and she could not forgive him.

To such of his offences as were indictable—tooth-gnashing, cursing, manhandling of his child—she had lost no time in drawing the Lord's attention: action (she had not a doubt of that) would shortly be taken in proper quarters. But she was still brooding, and brooding probably over what she felt she felt more keenly than could the Lord—her father's letting of her down. He had affronted, totally, her ideas for and her idea of him. Mania had burst out. He had misjudged her attitude, misconstrued her motives, gone so far as to call her a little so-and-so. In the course of attempting to twist her arm off he had blunderingly trodden upon her toe—and it had been that gross, blind inadvertence which most enraged her. For his true crime was having lost his head.

The outrage, of course, had been two-sided. What Fred had actually done to Maud was nothing to what he'd fancied she did to him. What the child had really been up to, one never would know; possibly she only half knew herself. But he imagined he knew: that was enough. If he'd felt baited, then in effect he was so. Seemingly she had taunted him with the letters—it was their, not her, power to torment over which Antonia had to ponder. So that was really the size of it, to him? How much had been dragged up, out of how many years? She rubbed at her forehead, fearing to know.

Reopening her eyes, Antonia found herself in the course of being regarded by Maud strangely; from, as it were, some new cosmic standpoint. This differed in an uneasy way from the child's more usual brief scrutinies in having evidently been going on for some time; nor, though caught in the act, did Maud now desist— the regard, which first had had the advantage of Antonia's minutes of abeyance, seemed to claim the right to continue, noted or not. Gladly though the other would have ignored it, she did not have it in her to do so for very long. "What are you sitting looking at me like that for?"

"I was thinking."

"And why, pray?"

"Mother says you were why I was born."

Antonia was stunned: she only so far recovered as to give a choking tug at her pearls.

"Yes; she says you could never leave well alone."

"*I* should have considered it, more, Fate."

"She says you always fall back on Fate sooner than face what you have done."

"Good God, Maud."

Maud gave a token frown.

"I mean to say, what next?—We're the instruments of each other's destinies right enough, but absolutely I won't agree that I caused you. Perfectly evidently you had to be—what the world had done to deserve you, one can't say. What has the world done to deserve most things?"

"Sinned," Maud said, not without satisfaction.

Antonia rolled off the bed, made for the wardrobe, tore off her shirt, and began to hunt for a fresh one, head-and-shoulders into the hanging garments' insufferable redolence of herself. Backing out again, dragging something tartan, she demanded: "And when do you and your mother have these chats?"

"When she's upset, sometimes."

Antonia stormed: "You should take no notice of people when they're upset."

"I don't, chiefly."

"And never quote them!"

"You and I upset her, Cousin Antonia."

"We've nothing else in common: you'd better go! I said 'for a minute,' and that's up.—Parading about psalm-singing outside my window! That was the plan—to move in on me, I suppose?"

Maud said: "I only wondered," in the tone of one who no longer does. She got off her chair with an air of accomplished purpose, seemed about to consider leaving the room, but instead took one or two steps to a point from which she could verify what was on the bedside table. She remarked a degree more matily: "Oh, you read the Bible." Antonia, fumblingly buttoning the new shirt, resented this in furious silence. "If you're not going downstairs," she declared finally, "I am."

"Or we both could," said Maud.

"No, I don't think so.—In your case, oughtn't it to
be tea-time?"

"It has been tea-time. No tea. Nobody's anywhere."

"How fast your curse is taking effect!"

Silence: Antonia could not but turn round. Maud,
now in touch with the bedside things, was puffing ash
off the bottle of sleeping pills, the better to read what
was on the label. She handled the bottle: pink capsules,
gone down in number, delinquent within it skidded and
slid. *"Leave those alone!"* Not so much reprobation as
sheer unmovedness was in the child's face as, after a
moment, she complied. "So," she seemed to remark,
"you are on the run. . . ." It *was* a child's face, tense
over the bones with skin, a high look of candour about
the forehead, awakeness widening the eye-sockets. Sin-
gularity, the unsludged clearness of a coin fresh from
the mint and not to be struck again, and that sort of
intentness hard not to identify with a kind of purity appeared in it; and among other attributes of the gaze was
fearlessness, only not more attractive because it was so
complete and, one might feel, justified. Nothing, or almost nothing, made Maud not young, not a child
throughout. Only, one missed in regard to her some
natural sensation within oneself—some fond perturbed-
ness or anxiety. In general one feels on behalf of children
the enemy menace of the future: love cannot hope to
go with them all the way, care cannot prevent what may

be to come. The younger the head, the dearer the child, the more we are given to apprehend the militating against it of ruthless forces. Children are our vulnerability: what may or may not be the striking power of years to be? Few are children for whom one feels no concern: Maud happened, however, to be one of them. Solicitude, in this case, went into reverse—what might the future not have to fear from her?

Her unmistakable content was moral force: how would she elect to wield it? She was Judgment, to which we must all be brought. She opened the cover of the Bible, twisted her head to read what was written inside, meditated upon that, let the cover fall. "Cousin Antonia?"

"That's enough," warned the other, rapidly starting for the door.

"*Was* Cousin Guy a good man?"

Antonia had got to the threshold: she snatched at the door-handle, making sure it would turn, before casting back her negligent-sounding answer: "I couldn't tell you."

"Or don't you know?"

But Antonia had fled the room, left the field to Maud. A minute later, anybody watching Montefort from the fields might have seen the child waving out of the window, making a summoning signal to Gay David, who waited below. Antonia meanwhile was at the stairhead—

hand on the shaking rail or shaking hand on the rail, she did not know which. It was true what Maud said: though it had long been tea-time, emptiness reigned throughout the historic house—all was suspended, except the question. Antonia, beginning to go downstairs, was met by the arid breath of outdoors—the door, standing as it had stood last night, open, let afternoon's bright shadows into the hall. One by one, across the view through the doorway, cattle were in a listless file proceeding towards the river woods: this, as the one movement, she stood intently watching from the foot of the stairs, where she had herself come to a stop.

It was the bottom of a well, this bottom of the stairs—she looked round to notice with what she shared it. Not yet quite aired out of the place was the reek of last midnight's burned-out lamp: dishevelment of horse-cloths upon the chair marked where Jane had sat, either found or lost. On the Gothic ledge of the hat-stand lodged the prayer-book, deposited on Maud's way through; and, next the prayer-book, a packet of letters tied with white ribbon. Antonia, picking the packet up, no more than glanced at the writing: she could now calculate what had been the movement of at least one man. Fred must have come in, gone out again, placed them here not knowing what else on earth to do with them.

IT WAS Peregrine, this time, who drove the Daimler. He had got it in at the gates, and was at a crawl proceeding along the avenue, which led, so far as his eye saw, only to desertion and further mountains, when Jane stepped out from behind a tree. They might have been meeting by appointment. He gave a nod and pulled up the car—the scene was sorrowfully sunny with yellow evening, haunted in ranks by beeches gone down one by one in gale after gale year after year. Nothing was to tell him that the disaster had not been all at a blow, yesterday—for indeed something bereft was in the quietness of the air—but that moss greened over the stumps, sunken, brambles had filled the outrooted hollows, and saplings, some of them at a height, already ventured into existence in the gaps between the surviving boles. Wide apart, shadows like trees fallen barricaded what was left of the avenue; and Jane's pink dress, tattered by light-and-shade, itself looked to him like a fragment—he had had no idea she was so poor. He leaned across, opened the passenger door, and said: "Hop in. Vesta wants to speak to you."

"You left the gates open."

"So?" asked Peregrine, glancing back.

"Cattle."

"Well, we'll be going out again. Can't turn here, though—if I go on, what happens?"

"Our house."

"Turn there, then," said Peregrine, unconcerned. "Let's get going, shall we?"

"*I'm* not coming," she told him, nicely enough.

"You're not doing anything," Peregrine pointed out. "And don't make difficulties, there's a good girl: this is something special."

"Something about last night?" she quickly asked—so betrayingly quickly that she had to do something to buy him off: she therefore slid into the seat beside him, making a point of not caring whether he answered, which he did not. They went on to make the loop-turn over the overgrown gravel, tires broadly crushing the white clover: at Montefort's door, open, and rows of windows he was courteous enough to glance; she also doing so—like a stranger. "Nobody about," he remarked to her, "that is, apparently." "No," she contradicted, "my cousin was in the hall." "Saw us, then?" "No, she was looking at something else." They tailed away again down the avenue.

Unhandily retying the gate chain-knot, he split a fingernail, which he showed her. "Oh dear," Jane responsibly said, though at the same time measuring his legs, their costly extension of chalk-striped flannel under the wheel, as though she considered him big enough to have done better. Later: "Why this cousin, always?" Peregrine asked, flicking the Daimler right, down the castle turning. "Are you an orphan?"

"No," she said, turning red.

"Terence had a theory you had a father."

"A father *and* mother." She interposed a hand between his observation and her blush; but need not have —he had returned to profile. He accelerated, explaining: "I'm under orders."

"Why didn't she send the chauffeur?"

"Harris? He's taken the van to Cork."

"Or come herself?"

"Oh, Vesta'd hardly do *that*. And anyhow we're not feeling too good today. As you'll see, we are a trifle fussed."

"Oh?"

"One thing and another, you know; one thing and another." Hedge-muffled miles went, negative, by, till once more he bestirred himself. "What d'you keep looking out for?"

"There's a white horse, often, on this road."

"Talking of that, a drink should do good." Speed, so far as blind corners allowed, rose. "Tootle-oo," he said to himself sadly; then to her: "Make any more hay today?"

"No; I—"

"No, I expected not.—What *were* you up to?"

"What you said."

"No, you were walking around in circles."

"Don't you, ever?"

"Somehow I never walk."

"Mayn't you get fat?"

"Somehow I never do." They approached the castle. "At one time," Peregrine volunteered, "I went round in circles a bit in my own mind."

Pyramidal the flowers were upon the piano, their scent exhausting what was left of the air. Never could drawingroom have been more empty. Jane, brought in by Peregrine, helplessly dropped on to the white sofa. The tray must be where it was before, for he had proceeded in that direction: from behind her, ice-noises splintered her memory. "And for you—what?" he wanted to know.

"Nothing!" she declared, over-loud, wildly, faced and confounded by the chimneypiece. Marble like a temple in a fever-swamp it stood, chilled off and haunted by the miasma—where, last night, *had* she rested her burning hand? Gone, gone, gone . . . The man in the room sighed, drank, sighed, put down his glass lingeringly. "You can't," he said, "mean that—absolutely nothing?"

"Why have I to be here?"

"To come back? You were terrific last night—anyone tell you?"

"My cousin supposed I was drunk.—Where *is* Lady Latterly, now I've come?"

"She'll be along," said Peregrine darkly. "Why? Don't you like it here any more?"

"Do you, always?" cruelly she returned. She was on the middle edge of the sofa, pressing her elbows to her sides: each end, above her, overpowering cushions stacked themselves up into lady-effigies.

"Suits me all right, more or less, on the whole," he supposed, lifelessly looking around his cage. "But a girl like you—a girl like you," he was moved to argue, "can't possibly want absolutely nothing. I mean, can't want *absolutely* nothing. Now, can you?" He vacillated over the rugs and parquet till he stood behind her, over the sofa. She looked up, backwards, to see why; whereupon fatalistically he drooped lower until he kissed her. She let him finish, then drew away—on the whole, thoughtfully. "Somehow this is a thing I never do in a car," he said. "Do you?"

"I don't know, really."

"Unconcentrated sort of a girl you are, aren't you?" Reflectively he went off to look for his glass. "I'm a bit off form today, which is not unusual, which is just as well.—What have *you* been doing?"

She seemed uncertain. "I went to sleep."

"Ever go to town?"

"I watched my mother having her hair cut."

"But what don't you know?" he restlessly asked, roaming her way again, glass in hand.

"Anything—apparently."

"You should, you know, sometime. It cheers one up."
He yawned.

"You yawn," she said, "almost like my father."

"Frustration, isn't it?—Certain you won't?"

"What?"

"*Not* a martini?"

She thought again. "Might that make this the same room?"

"As what?"

"Last night."

Peregrine thought it was worth trying. Jane, while he got to work with the shaker, put her fist to her forehead and lay back. She had been robbed, too short a time ago to have yet taken the measure of her loss. First, it had been the letters: their being gone had been a mystifying shock. Wakened by sounds of Maud in the afternoon, she had set out to visit them; though it had not been urgent, chiefly a reason for a stroll. In the sultry-scented inside of the elder, there the stone was, nothing at all to show it had been disturbed till she came to lift it—then, so completely no trace was to be found on the crushed-down, whitened roots of the grass that her first fear was, *had* they ever been there at all? Or had they conjured themselves into nothingness?—or stolen away by evaporation? Where, though, in that case, was her solid ribbon? No, no way out of it: she had had to know —vilely, the letters had been taken! But that, though bad, had been nothing more than the start, the foreshadowing of robbery to come. For the worst of loss is when it at the same time is an enlightenment—that is what is not to be recovered from; ignorance cannot be made good. She had lost her father, and twice over—lost him in not having known him until she'd lost him, lost him in the instant of a beholding. Yes, and in that comprehensive view through the arch she'd not only blundered upon a man and woman but perceived the packet upon her mother's wanton lap. Guy too, then, had finished his course here.

And come to nothing, her eyes told her—there in the lax dusk, under the incriminated shadow of the chestnut. Crisscrossed, the ribbon stayed as it was, white bow dishevelled, trifled with but no more. Disregarded, everything he had written! She's had her revenge like anything, thought the girl—and, even while she looked, the trophy slid down the taut blue cotton of the dress, failed to be stopped by a careless hand, fell. Dust rose where it fell, in a little puff, as unnoticed Jane fled back the way she'd come.

Anybody's game, she had thought, breathlessly slowing down into one of those pacing, far-ranging circles in whose course Peregrine had found her—anybody's game! Though which of them, dead man and living girl, had been the player, and which the played-with? Either way, Jane seemed doomed to know that this dallying and being-dallied-with had gone on long enough. The trouble was the aptitude for love—and, on

top of that, hadn't her mother said that one never knew
when or what at he might not laugh? And as for the
world, who knew when *it* might not start laughing behind its hand? . . . So here now was Jane, through the
instrumentality of Peregrine (acting under orders), biting upon the void of the whole story in this void, staled,
trite, and denying drawingroom—a goodbye is not what
it's said to be, her mother'd said. Jane suffered nothing
but dismay, but there are sometimes no bounds to that.
She once or twice hammered with her fist, to keep whatever it was down—then, rearing imperatively up among
the cushions, reached a hand out for the martini. "Do
you think," she put it to Peregrine, "I could be a me-
dium?"

"Far better try a job in a shop."

"No," she said, "I meant, without knowing?"

"Or model, or something, or so on, couldn't you?" He
brought the cocktail.

"Or bewitched, could I somehow possibly be?" She
drank, looking past him out of a window—"Here's,"
she said finally, "Lady Latterly." The chatelaine, wearing tapered slacks, was disappointedly trailing some
delphiniums; she disappeared to ascend the steps, then
entered. "Nobody ever told me!" she exclaimed in her
most persecuted tone, kissing Jane as though the moment for doing so were by now irretrievably gone. "I've
been so wondering," she confessed, "whether you'd possibly be an angel—I do hope you've told her?" she said

to Peregrine. She shelved the flowers and wrung her hands. "Then this *is* the end—where do I begin?"

"Ask her," suggested he, "if she knows Shannon."

"Well, I don't, anyway," said the girl.

"But you must!" cried Lady Latterly. "That airport."

"None of us fly."

"Well, you know," he said, "how people keep on arriving."

"Richard is not people," said Lady Latterly, dilating her nostrils. "He really feels things." She turned to Jane. "The thing is, I've had a telegram. . . ."

"Richard's arriving, out of the blue, ha-ha. Tomorrow."

"Don't be brutal, Peregrine."

"And tomorrow Vesta is going racing."

"What I'm so afraid of," said Lady Latterly, sitting down and pulling at a knee of her slacks, "is that he'll never feel quite the same again. Thousands of miles, to me, and then what?—no one. Not a face at the airport— when I was so, so fond of him."

"Vesta rather fears he may cut up. Be a bit stuffy, create, or so on."

"Might he?" Jane asked.

"Can't say; I don't know the type."

"He's such a boy," bemoaned Lady Latterly, biting at the tip of a finger with a ring on it, one eye on Peregrine. "Why does one let things happen?"

He did not seem to know or, alas, care. Jane was left to say: "Still, you'll send the car?"

"No, Peregrine and I'll need the car, you see. No, it comes down to Harris and that unkind van. Unless—" added Lady Latterly, fixing Jane for an instant of concentrated suspense "—unless *you* were an angel and went along?"

KATHIE entered the Montefort kitchen from the yard, knocking sweat from her forehead with the back of her hand. Her arms ached from the buckets by means of which, all afternoon, she had been assisting in scooping the shallow river up into the barrel of the water-cart. Everywhere having run dry above, the cart had had to make several journeys, down and up the zigzag track— she had run ahead while it creaked on its last ascent. Nothing did she like better than an emergency, the doing of work which was not her own—she came indoors again, now the fun was over, with something of a sinking of the heart. Trickily dark was it indoors, after hours out in the water glare—there, however, really *was* Miss Antonia, kaleidoscopic in tartan, in the act of trying to hook the lid off the range. The range kept its attacker back by radiating a massive heat, intolerable this afternoon, from every part of its rusted surface; and Miss Antonia had further hampered herself by taking to it the wrong, short poker. This, when Kathie came in, she hid behind her as though surprised in the act of murder. "What on earth do you want?" she said.

To be asked what she wanted never put Kathie out; what she dreaded was their asking what she was doing. Miss Antonia's unwillingness to account for what *she* was doing was most interesting; for never had she been known to so much as look into a pot or shift a kettle. The girl answered simply by making a bee line for the spring-water crock under the shelf, and thirstily gulping straight from the dipper. "It would parch you," she stated, patting her chest, "to keep at it handling water you couldn't touch. The old cattle fouled what's left in the river.—Will I do that for you, miss, whatever it is?"

"No." Thrown out, as one is by a change of mind, queered in will, as one is by an intervention, Antonia stood fecklessly tossing the packet of letters in the air. "Read," she at random inquired, "can you?"

"Never set eye on *those*," declared Kathie, swiftly. Untying her sacking apron, she watched. "Miss, that's a bit of ribbon you'd never burn?"

"Who said I was going to burn anything?—Want it, to tie up your bonny brown hair?"

The idea sent Kathie's hands round her head. "Well, I'd be glad of it, but that it's Miss Jane's.—Did you notice her making loops in the castle motor? They were at it when I was coming out of the wood." Kathie, in search of another apron, tugged in turn at each of the dresser drawers. "Fire's the finish." She glanced at the dormant range. "If you spared the ribbon, mightn't you still be sorry? It should have taken patience to write all *that* down. Whoever was it, I wonder, was so clever?" The girl diverted the question by a look at herself in the small glass over the sink.

"Mr. Guy. You ever heard of him?"

"No, miss," said Kathie in her most safe-side manner. "Unless I heard he was dead, poor man?"

"You might have. His photograph's in the hall."

"You took *that* one, miss?"

"Oh dear no, alas."

"Then he should be one of the family?"

"Owned this place."

"It's a pity he was cut short." Kathie, however, spoke distractedly—she had made a professional rush at the kitchen table and was going over what was upon it. "Look at that," she burst out, "nobody took their tea! What became of them? I left the pot out, look, and the canister with it, and here they are, high and dry! What's this mystery?—was there trouble?"

"Miss Maud put a curse on the house." Having chucked the letters on to the table, Antonia used both hands to stuff her shirt in, as, turning away, she made for the door. "The long and the short of it is, they're out."

"Wait," cried the girl, "you forgot the writing!"

"No, I did not," contradicted the other, from the echoing passage.

"What's it here for, then?"

"Whoever's next, I suppose."

"Miss—?"

"What?" chafed Antonia.

"Is it wicked writing?"

"Look, if you like!"

"Ah, I'd never dare!"

But the protest was almost mocking. Kathie had followed Antonia out: she stood, arms tight-folded, staring. A conflict of expressions was on her face—resentment and excitement at being tempted, guile, just not childish, and calculation. Like a grandmother, she sucked in her mouth—while joy, pure joy at the notion of such temerity, startled her eyes open to their widest. She let her breath right out, got none back. Flattered, she nonetheless felt misprised, invited as being of no account: of account *was* her virtue, and she knew it—warily she stood and measured the lady who'd challenged her to engage it, perhaps lose it. "I wouldn't care to mix myself up in that," she declared, though still with her head on one side. Antonia turned away, saying: "Don't, then," by which Kathie was left forlorn—"I'd hardly know," she said sadly, "whether I should."

"They've run their course," said Antonia, over her shoulder, starting away down the passage, "this last day or two."

"This last day or two," argued the girl, "there wasn't a thing wrong with us but the weather. Heat, you can't

overlook: they say it was never like this till now—
though *I* was never in any other house. Anything's natural enough, I daresay, here.—Or should be," she added
with some misgiving, a fidget from one to the other
foot. "Only, for goodness sake, what's come up? I'm
sure I'd never care to stay where there'd been a curse."

"That was Miss Maud's fun."

"She's a tormentor," agreed Kathie.

Stupendously, all at once, she began to giggle. She
saw daylight, and it was too much for her, it convulsed
her—so much so that, ripping her arms apart, she had
to beat them upon the air. Bent in two, she vomited
laughter; though also, mortified by the exhibition, she
let out penitent sobs and moans. This brought Antonia
back on her tracks, to ask: "What on earth's as funny as
all that?"

"N-nothing, miss," admitted Kathie. She hiccupped.

"Then don't hiccup."

"Only, tormenting and teasing is half the fun—"

Antonia shifted her black spectacles. Her saying nothing emboldened Kathie to finish: "—when it's a lovely
man."

"That's a wicked thought."

Kathie nursed it, liking it all the better. "There could
still," she said, "be some terrible joke on us."

"Nothing in this house passes without comment,"
reflected Lilia, far from unhappily, seated on the edge

of her bed cutting her toenails. Coming indoors just now, through the hall, she'd been swept on upstairs by the conviction that the hum to be heard in the stone passage could have arisen only because of her. "Oh, Antonia?" she called demandingly, upon a footstep's threatening to pass her door, which she'd left ajar.

"Then so there you are," conceded the other, coming no further in than she must.

"And why not?" asked Lilia, contemplating her right foot in balance upon her left knee.

"No idea why not," confessed Antonia, noticing that the bedroom since Fred's absence had gone on to spawn every kind of knick-knack. "Merely that Maud went without her tea."

"Oh, she did? Then why ever couldn't Kathie?"

"Filling the water-cart."

"Far too much," pronounced Lilia, though now remotely, "goes on down at that river, and always has." She went to work again with the fragile scissors—snipping, shaping, testing for smoothness with the pad of her thumb.

"One good cut," quoth Antonia, "deserves another—your hair this morning." She appeared to feel she could now go. "Or did you," she asked reluctantly, "want to speak to me?"

"Yes. I thought I *might* go to London."

"Whatever for?"

Lilia lifted her eyelids. "You told me I should. You said that I ought to."

"Well, it's exceedingly good of you, but *I'm* going, now."

"Are you? How fast you make up your mind."

"Nothing to how fast you change yours. You screamed the place down this morning, at the very idea."

Lilia said: "Ah, but that was this morning."

"What induced you to make such an awful scene?"

"I don't recall," said the other calmly.

"Well, I do. It was nice for Jane."

"Jane's not by now so particular," observed Lilia, stooping, supporting her bust with one arm, to gather up slivers of toenail from the carpet. "Taking her with you, shall you be?"

"Certainly. It's high time she went to work."

"Otherwise, only be getting into mischief," assented Lilia, "or don't you think so?" A pause ensued, while she raised herself up—she then deliberately turned her head in Antonia's direction: the women's eyes met. Unflinchingly Lilia said: "What did it matter? You knew Guy was untrue to me."

Antonia gave a rub at her lower lip, glanced at the blood-guilty lipstick on the finger. "Then you knew too, then."

"Yes; at the last," Lilia said in a lightened, relieved tone, putting on the same shoe Fred had put on for her.

"How—I'd like to know?"

"I could hear you both, at that station."

"Oh, you mean only *that*."

"What more could I wish?"

"You carried it off well, then, Lilia, I must say!"

"It still meant something to me to be true to him."

"I suppose it did: what a bore you were."

"It was all I had."

"Still, you went too far—letting him waste your life."

"*He* did not," replied Lilia, finding the other shoe. She put it on, rose, stood and balanced in both as though on skates, then went across, cast the slivers into the grate, and drew a chiffon scarf out of a drawer. Sailing past Antonia, she left the bedroom. She trod down the stairs, seeming oblivious of the other hard at her heels. Antonia, at last coming abreast, begged to know: "What are you doing now?"

"We thought of going out for a spin."

"You and who?"

"I and Fred—for a blow of air," amplified Lilia, fanning her brow to show the need. She opened the fence gate into the elsewhere of the evening: up stood the obelisk over floating light; sunset kindling the belt of trees dissolved into others the faint elder—from which like a cry came the sadness of something gone. "Like we sometimes used to," Lilia continued.

"Fred needs a blow of air?"

"It was his idea."

The two stood waiting, backs to the fence. "Fred bringing the car round?" Antonia asked.

"I expect so. I like to start from the front."

Antonia suggested: "Almost a pity to go to London?"

Lilia smiled: "Oh no, I should like to—now."

"Now's the time, you feel?"

"For about a week."

"The week will seem long," said Antonia thoughtfully.

"To me?" asked Lilia, surprised.

"Oh, no, no. No, to those left behind."

Lilia said: "Yes. That was what I thought."

A N T O N I A and Maud, at supper in silence, were waited upon by Kathie, also either subdued or preoccupied— that was to say, the servant came in from time to time with after-thoughts, sliced beetroot, seed cake, an unset junket, and so on, which she recommended to notice without a word. Once Maud, as an experiment, rang the handbell, after which no more happened, but that the red-walled diningroom, blinds lowered as though at midday, went on filling with premature dusk.

Jane, when she did so, entered without warning and with bravado. "Whoo!" vaunted the girl, seizing a jug and pouring out milk for herself with a big splash, "I thought *I* was late!" She referred in no other way to the empty head and foot of the table.

Maud got up, sped to the wireless in the corner, and

turned a knob—out came blood-up laughter, which, thanks to the force of the new battery, blasted its way round and round the room, bringing the instant look of a quarry, terror, mortification, to Jane's face. Maud, mind set at rest, switched off—"It's not," she explained to them, "nine o'clock yet."

"I could have told you that," expostulated her sister.

"Well, I know now."

"It was five to eight," went on Jane in a firm, tense voice, "when I left the castle." Antonia, already so sunk in thought as to have reacted in no way to the wireless, merely went on sipping whisky-and-water. "The drive," the girl added, "takes twenty minutes."

"Then where's the Daimler?" asked Maud accusingly.

"It? Oh, I was dropped at the gate."

"Oh."

"You've been drinking again," said Antonia, obliged to arouse herself, sending a look, crooked, across the table.

"And I was seduced, this time," said Jane, defiantly helping herself to beetroot, which no one had so far touched.

"Well, that doesn't matter: we're going away tomorrow."

"No—how can we be?"

"Because I say so."

"But how can you possibly say we are?" The girl turned white and put down her fork.

"Time we did."

"Is this on my account?"

Antonia shrugged her shoulders.

"But Antonia—everything's over!" The entrenched presence of Maud could not but put a constriction on Jane's lips; and as things were, perhaps it was better so. Yet a hampered anger, anger at being hampered, rose in her breast. What she'd done—and what *had* she done?— was being made unspeakable by not being spoken. Women had framed her up—and that went for Maud, too. "You needn't worry, you know, Antonia," she aloofly said—aloofly, yet with an infinity of scorn, though for whom or what, or why, it could not be known. "Everything's over."

"What, thanks to Maud?"

Maud looked down her nose. Jane, turning to her— to her more than upon her, for this was largeness rather than anger—said: "Oh, then it *was* you? It was only you."

"Maud's," said Antonia, "been through deep waters."

"I'm afraid," said Jane, "I don't know what deep waters are.—You can't possibly mean to go back to London?"

"Many of us may be going—your mother, too."

"She'd rather die, she said," said the girl at once.

"But that," pointed out Antonia, "was this morning."

"*Now* why is she going?" Maud asked with justified coldness, for this was the first she'd heard of it. "Leaving Father?"

"Yes. For a week."

The child, though not with surprise, said: "Oh." She added: "And, I suppose, me."

"Antonia, what a day you seem to have had!" cried the girl, bravely mocking on. Though, turning her face from the two others, she was forced to behold the plate, knife-and-fork, cup-and-saucer at the head of the table vainly awaiting Fred. She declared, in a tone which defied the world to detect in it any loss of her golden confidence: "Then *I* ought to stay and look after him!"

"Just when had you thought of beginning to earn your living?"

"Not, I do hope, while it's so hot." But Jane suddenly ate some beetroot, as though an end to sustenance loomed in sight. "Though in a way I'd have thought I already did.—Does this mean we're stony again, Antonia? In that case, who's going to pay for Mother?"

"What d'you mean, you thought you already did?"

Rising, Jane walked round the table and to a window: she gave a twitch to the yellow blind, considered whether to raise it, but did not. Passing behind Antonia's chair, she repeated the performance with the two others, each time with more indecision. Distantly staying where this had left her, somewhere in the embrasure of the third, she at last replied to Antonia: "I've been a pleasure."

Antonia took time to lean back—she recrossed her knees, then asked: "What makes you think that?"

"I don't *think* it," steadily said the girl.

"Anything," said the other, holding up a cigarette as an instance, "can be a pleasure. Taking pleasure, that's what needs genius—idiot! Come and sit down."

"Antonia, why are you so hard on me?"

Antonia repeated: "Come and sit *down!*"

"Why?" deliberated the girl, with that new air of making her own terms.

"Can't stand anybody behind my back."

"Except Guy?"

The other, ignoring that, said: "As you ought to know, by now."

Jane, reflectively twiddling the blind-cord, said: "I was looking for a hat—I thought. Two nights ago, when I went into that attic."

"You blunderer! There was due to be a crisis," said Antonia, "for us all."

"I never *have* been so happy!" confessed the girl, with a rush letting the blind up. Ruefully and ecstatically, as though, almost, for the last time before a death, she breathed in the stocks and roses in the garden: the window was open. "Fool as I've looked, fooled as I've been! —Antonia, when shall I *be* so happy?"

Antonia, drily and out of solitude, said: "You, Jane? Why, any day—tomorrow!"

"*It is going,*" breathed Maud, "*to be Nine O'Clock.*"

Fanatical, Maud was crouched in the corner, one knee kneeling before the wireless. Her clutch was upon the knob, her stare close to the premonitory silence. Now, dogmatically and beautifully, the chimes began, completed their quarters, ended. Maud gnawed her lip and increased the volume. At the full, the first of the whanging blows struck down upon quivering ether, the echo swelling as it uprose. Repetition, fall of stroke after stroke where stroke after stroke had already fallen, could do no more than had been done: once was enough. From the first, the room was a struck ship— hither, thither slithered the thoughts and senses; the windows, like port-holes careened over, appearing actually to fill up. The sound of Time, inexorably coming as it did, at once was absolute and fatal. Passionless Big Ben.

The reminder, after so long, came with an accumulation of all force, and eloquence more than could be borne, demanding finally the reckoning. One was harkening to an ultimatum. The term had been set, and the term extended, again, again and again, while useless the fate of nations went on preparing; and for what culmination, and for what? Rubbed-weary passions had had their say, leaving nothing said. But now came Now—the imperative, the dividing moment, the spell-breaker—all else was thrown behind, disappeared from reality, was over. Time swooped as it struck—and Antonia, hearing each felling blow, flinched once: who can flinch nine times? Turning, she sought with her eyes for Jane, as though there were something she was forced to confess—to Jane, who should be and still was standing where she had last stood; though, telepathically awed, at bay for no reason that she knew, the girl had backed back into a window-curtain. Together braving the sound, while it continued to not cease, the two looked almost humbly away from each other. "And I *shall* never see Antonia again," Jane thought. "Something has happened. Somehow she's gone.—She's old."

"That was loud, surely?" Jane said to Maud in a tone of shock, upon the expiration of the last stroke.

The child crouched lower, heard out the final echo, then switched off—disdaining to answer, disdaining, as ever, to hear the news. The room righted its balance, causing objects to seem to be slipping back into what had been their position: on the avenue could be heard at a crawl the Ford, the two in it ekeing out their return —Jane the more hurriedly left the window. Coming behind Antonia, knowing the proscription to be suspended, she slid her arms into a clasp round the pearl-choked neck and, pressing the embrace closer, leaned round and brought her lips to the tarnished cheekbone. Under that dwelling kiss, at once comforting and beseeching, Antonia eased back her head on to Jane's breast. The girl then sighed, the woman said nothing. Simultaneously, both looked at the head of the table. As ever, it was after Guy had gone that he most nearly was to be seen. Gone for good, he had never appeared more clearly than he did at this last.

Heard to swerve, the Ford went through the arch to the back. Maud, reseated, took more cake. Kathie, in turn alerted by the activities in the yard, made no less haste to come in with the tray of tea. "In any event," she said, "they'll be wanting this," and plumped it down on the sideboard. "Shouldn't I bring the lamp?" The fact that she spoke went with some other alteration in her mien: she was tuned right up again, newly adorned in *some* way, and above all conscious, daringly conscious, of this herself—but she'd vanished before one could pin the impression down. Antonia, who had instinctively risen when the car's engine stopped, sat down again; Jane, retrospectively blushing, reclined again, sideways, in her place opposite. All acquiescently waited. Lilia's entrance, accompanied by Fred, was thus robbed of none of its due effect.

She, Lilia, unwound the chiffon scarf from her hair, hardly less languorously observing that she'd no notion what time it was. She, though without petulance, rang the handbell. "Close it feels in here, after that air!" Drawing the biscuits towards herself, she smiled and began to nibble at one. "There's a difference, however— you said so, didn't you, Fred?"

He pronounced: "Yes. The sky's coming over." He walked to the head of the table and sat down. "Hello?" he said idly, perceiving Jane.

She asked: "Not *clouding* over?"

"There'll be a change for rain.—Tea, is there?"

Jane brought the teapot, saying: "Oh dear. Tomorrow?"

"I said a change, not rain." Fred, stirring his tea, was struck by another thought, looked along at Maud, gave an outright guffaw. Sobering down again, he went on: "Though we're stuck if there's not, dam' soon." He eyed Jane, asking: "Any objection?"

"I'm going, I think, to Shannon."

"Nothing to stop you."

"Unless," pleaded the girl, across to Antonia, "unless we're going away?"

"I'm not going anywhere if it rains.—But how can it?" Antonia added.

"Fred deserves rain," Lilia replied, casting the ceiling a provocative glance. Yet the idea of an end to this golden spell made an unwilling shiver run up her arms. "It's been too hot, you'll admit," she said somewhat loudly. No one assented—upon which she felt herself ringed around by conspirators. "What have you all been doing," she challenged them, "sitting here in the dark?"

"Kathie's," said Maud, noncommittal, "bringing the lamp in."

"Simpler to put the blinds up, *I* should have thought."

"Why, yes; I suppose so," agreed Antonia. Jane was busy; she was bringing her father the dish of brawn. Her movements were swift and accomplished; she did not look at him.

"Shannon, did I hear you say?" asked Antonia.

"Vesta's van's got to go there."

In came the lamp, steadied by Kathie. She, bending to set it down, let be seen a brightly-white satin bow perked atop of her hair, which in crisps fell over the snood. Around the table breaths one by one were drawn, but to be held—not even Maud spoke. The maid at length stole a look at Jane. "I saved it," she said, aside. "No harm?"

"None."

Satisfied, Kathie centred the lamp, moving a dish here or a plate there. The glare from the globe, placed as it was, hit Fred directly upon the forehead, making him seem likely to frown: otherwise, he seemed to have no complaint. Lilia's expression, however, became more mystified: the cause was known only when Kathie'd left them. "And yet," she said, "she objects to wearing a cap."

"Why's Vesta's van going to Shannon?" resumed Antonia.

Jane said, looking startled: "To meet someone."

"That should be very nice. Vesta going?"

"Oh, no. Vesta is going racing."

"*That* will be very nice."

"You do think it will?" asked the girl, anxious.

"It will be a change."

"I suppose it will.—But suppose it rains?"

XI

THE film over the sky had been there since morning, dull as a ceiling. Not a cloud formed in it; it was cloud itself.

One had woken to find the sun gone, earth greener in the abated light—while into the air as it cooled off an almost rank smell rose from the grass and nettle-dark woods, already moist by anticipation. Everything on the plateau around Montefort, to which the mountains, ink-blue, had drawn nearer, stood out meaningly—one was aware of trees as each a great individual thirsting plant, and of white-grey rocks breaking the surface as porous limestone. And the limestone gave out into the sunlessness a glare, left behind by yesterday. The obelisk on its rise looked like the enlarged photograph of a monument.

Gone from all things was the mirage-like shimmer, the blond hue. One saw the darker constituents of the landscape and, where mountains were not, measured its flow into distances which were no less distinct. The clearness was hypnotic, as was the stillness—which, that of the change, was more intent than that of the heat. The uncanny imminence of rain hushed almost every other sensation. Today seemed not yet to be reality: one had so far no more than passed or been sent on out of one deep dream into another—more oppressive, more lucid, more near perhaps to the waking hour.

The morning was spent waiting either for rain to fall or the van to come—the latter was not actually due until two o'clock, but long before could be felt impending. The postman, making one of his rare calls, aware that he delivered nothing important, also looked speculatively at the sky. In the main, the departure of the fine spell, so far followed by nothing else, gave this beginning of the day an atmosphere at once unsettled and negative, tense and neutral. Jane, knowing that she was sooner or later to go away, spent time in her room going through her things—she took down and dusted a suitcase, and re-whitened her sandals to go to Shannon. Putting the sandals outside her window to dry, she saw her mother out there in the garden: Lilia had come down late, still wore a wistaria *crêpe* kimono, and was slowly taking a look around. "So," she remarked, hearing Jane above her, "your father *was* right. Still, it may hold off."

The girl said oh yes, she thought it should.

"Heat more often terminates in a thunderstorm," said Lilia.

"We're being let off light, then!"

"Still, I should take a coat.—It struck me to wonder if Maud could go."

Jane all but knocked a sandal off the window-ledge. "Oh!" she protested.

"I don't," her mother explained, "you see, intend taking her to London. So she'd enjoy this.—Whom are you to meet?"

"A cast-off lover of Vesta's. Why?"

"Then why object to having Maud in the van?"

"She bumps about so," said Jane vaguely.

"And what a position for you! You may find you are far from sorry to have Maud."

"I'll have Harris."

"Well, we shall have to see," Lilia declared, with an air of dealing with forces beyond control. Again she gazed round. "Only look at those mountains—*those* mean rain, if you like! And Antonia has rheumatism this morning.—I suppose I ought to slip on a frock."

"What a pity; you look like a Geisha Girl."

"What, do I?" mused Lilia. Jane left the window.

Sounds were magnified by the listening air—a bird in the woods, the creak of a yard door, a dog barking away in a distant farm. The girl pulled from her wardrobe the muslin dress, shook it out, contemplated the stained hems, wondered. She asked herself why she had cut the sleeves out—they were the beautiful thing about it, she now knew; sunshiney, softly flopping while she'd made play with a letter beside the obelisk. What had she mutilated? And now to the muslin the smell of banishment had returned—the pastness from which Antonia'd shrunk, the dregs of aroma from the exhausted sachet. Jane crushed up to her face the defeated stuff, desired to wetten it with a tear, but could not: bundling the dress up, she thrust it into the bottom of the wardrobe. She took from a hanger a candy-striped blazer, not worn yet, and tried it on. The cool day possibly could turn cold.

"Anything I could do before we go?" she was standing asking, some minutes later, at Antonia's bedside. The other, tweed cape over her shoulders, sat half-up, rapidly writing on a pad. "Go?" she said. "I haven't made any plans. Yes, we might as well—I suppose?"

"I supposed we were," said the girl patiently.

Antonia dashed down a few words more, then put the pad aside, face down. Aloud she reflected: "It's cheaper here."

"I know, Antonia; but you get bored."

"What you mean is, I drink more?—If it weren't for money, we could get off to Spain: what I need is sun."

In view of all, Jane could not help smiling.

"Or almost anywhere, really," went on Antonia, grandly rearranging the cape.

"I was to work," pointed out the girl.

"Oh, it may not come to that!"

"Haven't *you* got anything to do, Antonia? Anything that you must do and get money for, I mean to say, like you used to have?"

"Of course I have," said the other angrily. "What d'you imagine? So much too much, in point of fact, that what I need to do is think.—Which I was doing," she added, "when you came in. *You'll* dislike work; you've no idea what it is."

"Well, I've been educated; that's bad enough.—And after all, Antonia"—Jane indicated the outside world easily, almost eagerly—"summer's over!"

"Don't you be too sure," advised the other, eying the blazer. "Now, go.—When do you start?"

"At about two."

Antonia, again alone, tore the sheet off the pad and wrote no more. She groaned and looked blankly out of a window. Where to go, how to get there, and why? London? Tenants were in her flat. As to work, what next? She had refused commissions: ideas, where were they? Had she run right out? She thought: "I was better when I was miserable. What's killed misery?—what will kill me: age." Sometimes now in the nights in her vitals a cold hand felt about for the weak spot; death could be waiting to find its way in. Waiting for her to crack, or to lose nerve.

To do her justice, she had tried most things. It was

her former husband to whom she'd been writing when interrupted. So soon over, so long ago had been the try at marriage that it was not a substantial memory. Antonia's ever having been married seemed so unlikely, so out of character, that few who knew her believed that story. Lilia, as she herself remarked, would not have done so had she not known the facts: what she certainly did not wonder at was the failure—this she would tend to revert to, from time to time, when in danger of being put upon by Antonia, in a manner which continued to be galling. Apart from that, there had not been loss of face—on either side, one was glad to be sure. Alex had been (indeed, still was) his name. He never thought less amiably of Antonia, would have been happy to lend her money, and had, last time they'd happened to meet, offered her the use of his flat in Paris—that was, when he should not be in it. So this morning she'd woken with the idea of writing—and why not?—to ask him whether the flat was empty: it might suit her. Or, *was* that the reason she had woken with the idea of writing? "My heavens," she thought, "have I come to this?" She reached around in a panic for the half-written sheet and contemptuously crunched it into a ball. In a minute or two it rolled off the bed.

This insane London spree for Lilia, what would it cost? *She'll* soon find her way round Derry and Toms.

"Paying up, I keep on," fumed Antonia. "My fault, not having called her bluff at the start." Start—when had it started? Bluff, had it been, really, ever? "Haystack, yes; but the needle was in it somewhere. She and I knew the truth—Guy *did* love her, like it or not. So why go back over that?"

He came back, through Jane, to be let go. It was high time.

When that clock struck, it said: "Enough!"

"But that being so," thought Antonia, "we shall hardly know each other. For what now?" She slid down in bed, drawing the cape with her for extra cover. The future was now the bore; which was to say, the future was now the thing—it could do it no harm, however, to be left in abeyance a short time longer; till Jane, for instance, was back from Shannon. Who knew what might not decide itself? Or, as against that, nothing at all might happen, which would be a kind of decision too. The day itself might do no more than look more and more like rain—indeed, the air by assuming a false tense glint was turning the grass livid with thwarted longing; and so, considered Antonia (herself now desiring nothing), it would do it no harm to stay. Remembering that on Jane's account (and Maud's also, it now seemed) the dinner-hour had been put forward, she thought she should soon probably get up: her sense of reprieve as to all else made the prospect less trying than usual.

Three barometers hung in different parts of the hall; Jane idly passed from one to another, tapping. "When," she asked as Antonia came downstairs, "did any of these last go, I wonder?"

"Not in my time, I fancy. We never looked at them."

"*This* one possibly could be—or could it? It says 'Fair' —but then you've got rheumatism, haven't you?" said the girl reproachfully.

"No, not, after all. And anyway rain doesn't stop flying."

"No, but it's not so nice. And think of arriving!"

"By the way, why's he arriving if he's cast-off?"

"Oh dear—how do you know?"

"You and your mother were simply shouting."

"The awful thing," said Jane, in a burst of confidence, "is that he doesn't know. He wasn't cast off in time to stop him. And *I* don't even know where he's coming from: I suppose Harris does."

"Harris should have the flight-number."

Jane leaned her shoulder against the distempered wall, beside the hopeful barometer, which hung on the other side of the clock from Guy's photograph. "I seem," she said anxiously and despondently, "to have started saying such awful things."

"—That wall will come off on to your blazer!"

Jane moved, gave the shoulder a backward brush, but went on: "Like saying I'd been seduced. That was only Peregrine."

"Today you're taking a bodyguard?"

"Nothing more's been actually said, but . . ."

"Like me to try a word with your mother?"

"Oh, no, no—no, I don't want some awful fuss. And after all—" Jane gave a baffled sigh—"why should I care? What does it matter?"

T H E V A N was with them when least expected. One moment not there, the next it was, with an air of having been there always. It took part in the landscape, filling the foreground. Maud was the first to issue from the house; Harris touched his cap, but so far said nothing. The child prowled round the vehicle, looking at and into it at all angles: the seating inside reminded her of a small church. "You could put a horse in this," she said, "if necessary."

"Well, it isn't normally used for that, miss."

Lilia, next upon the scene, turned a warning though weak look upon Maud before saying: "Good afternoon, Harris." The entire ambience of their meeting was different this time—for one thing, she knew his name. "Do you think," she asked, "it's going to rain?"

"I could not say, madam," he replied, in his English

voice of utter authority. "Might hold off. Still, it's a change since yesterday."

Lilia agreed. She went on to say: "I'm afraid my daughter's not quite ready. She can't find something."

"We're ahead of time, by a bit," said Harris, untroubled. He turned in the other direction his hinged head. "Quite an interesting monument you've got there. Caught my attention the other evening." Fred having opportunely appeared, Lilia was able to say to him: "Harris has been admiring the obelisk." She linked her arm maritally through Fred's. "I wish I could remember its origin—surely it must have had one, didn't it, Fred?"

"Chap put it up in memory of himself," said he, with a glance at the thing, for the first time struck by it.

"What, while he was still alive?" marvelled Lilia. "Rather peculiar, surely? What was his name?"

"Couldn't tell you."

"Oh, then he *is* forgotten!"

During the pause, Antonia joined the group, was asked, looked bored, and supplied the name. She carried her cup and was drinking coffee. "Married the cook," she went on, "went queer in the head from drinking and thinking about himself, left no children—anyway, no legits. So this place went to his first cousin.—Where on earth's Jane? Hurry her up."

"Harris," said Lilia, "says there's plenty of time."

"Well, there's *time*, madam."

Fred, disengaging himself from Lilia for this purpose, was to be the next to walk round the van; this he did in a sceptical although still open-minded manner, looking underneath it, which had not been done before. Finally saying to Harris: "Mind if I do?" he flung open the bonnet. "Hmmm," he remarked, standing back, "how d'you find her?"

"So-so," said Harris, and cleared his throat. He was looking away again, this time not at the obelisk but at the rise on which it stood, and something in the nature of his attention made each blade and leaf upon the incline stand out stereoscopically sharply. When Harris said: "Clover, I shouldn't wonder?" the others heard him without surprise. "Mind if I look?—I could do with a bit of luck." Speaking, he swung himself from the van and, concentrated, set off upon his quest—except for his chauffeur's cap he was not in uniform but wore a sort of a compromise get-up, dark coat, groom's breeches. He struck, in fact, a note that went with the van; and this, with the milieu in which he found himself, accounted no doubt for the jauntiness, the foreboding and distant egalitarianism of his manner, which was at no point ever not correct, for he would not so far yield to them as to have it otherwise. All watched. He proceeded unerringly to a point some three feet from the base of the monument, stopped, stooped, plucked, straightened his back again. "My God," said Antonia, "he's found one!"

Harris started back to them, twirling the four-leaved clover. Slowing down on his way, he with care began working the weak stalk into his button-hole. Maud had meanwhile seized the occasion to settle herself on the van's front seat: she had with her her plastic raincoat, in whose pocket could be seen to be folded the pixie hood, and less visibly was accompanied by Gay David. She looked patronizingly at her family through the wind-screen. Harris, reoccupying the driver's place, said: "Well, look who's here," without enthusiasm.

"I wondered," said Lilia, hastening up, "whether you or her ladyship would object if my little girl were to go with you? She's never seen an aeroplane."

"Yes I *have*," said Maud, perfectly furious.

Harris said: "Well, I couldn't speak for her ladyship."

Jane in white, blazer over her arm, appeared in the door of Montefort saying: "Father?" at which Fred half-comprehendingly turned. The girl said: "Only, I'm off. Goodbye," and, ducking her head, made a blind bridal rush past him into the van. Harris reached forward to touch the starter.

But Jane immediately cried: "Wait!" She wound down a window and leaned out, abashed but saying "An-tonia . . ." in a low urgent summoning tone which brought the other alongside, fretted by more of this in the sunless glare. And Jane, as though all of Antonia's faculties must somewhere be in the dark of those twin pools, spoke directly into the sunglasses: "I *do* know who they were to," she said very hurriedly. "Shall I tell you?"

"What have you been doing?"

"Burning them."

"What, with this at the door?" asked Antonia, kicking a tire of the van. "And, what do you mean? They were burned last night."

"No; Kathie got frightened. She found a name in them."

"Oh?" said Antonia.

Jane gave the unknown name, naturally adding: "So who was she?"

"I don't believe I remember," said Antonia. She stepped back, saying: "You'd better start," with a nod at Harris. The van moved. The girl's last cry as she fell away from the window, against Maud, was: "Anyway, that *was* who it was. So tell Mother!"

"What?" asked Lilia. "What is it? What has Jane been doing?"

The van, turning, was out of earshot. Antonia, whether idly or madly, said: "Burning those letters from Guy to you."

Lilia said, by reflex: "She should have asked me." Her hand climbed fumblingly to her throat. "Sure, are you —*sure* that was what she said?"

Antonia, faced by that ancient face of youth, had not the heart to turn back. "Yes," she said.

With a dazed lost sob Lilia ran back to Fred. Though he never would be Guy, never quite the same.

Watching the van drive away, bearing the children, the three stood—Antonia outside the fence, Fred and Lilia framed in the doorway. This was an echo, a second time—second time of what? Wedding afternoon. All was repeated almost exactly—summer emptiness darkening along the edges, hypnotic sky. Yes, and today could, if one wished, be counted an anniversary; for the Danby wedding had been, had it not, on much such a day as this was, near the end of a June. Left behind in that doorway the pair had stood, watching Antonia drive away in their wedding taxi, free of them. Those two she had forced to their bridal doom; she had left them to it, and to what? But the fact was there had been no going *away;* one is never quite quit of what one has done. What had they done to her?—they had sucked her back. Nor, as Fred said, had she been as clever as she thought: her decree, her overweeningness, her apparent will had done no more than implement waiting nature— they were to marry, whether or not. There had been compulsion, yes; but she was subject no less than they: Guy's death, even, had been contributary to Jane's birth. And so, what was Jane for? Beautiful, yes; but why?

The two in the door, watching the van drive off, had

resumed that air they wore on their wedding day, that
air of having been thrown together. It was the former
look, which it had taken Antonia twenty-one years to
fathom, not so much of misgiving as of subservience.
What might be the acquaintanceship of their bodies
seemed by this moment to be dissolved to nothing; for
there, being carried away in the van, went all there had
been to show for it: Jane, Maud. Antonia wondered
what thought, if indeed any, at this moment was in their
joint mind—she would never know. She *had* never
known them—that is, so far as thought goes. But she had
felt them; she felt them now. She had pictured and was
now picturing them—one does not need absence to do
that. "And indeed perhaps," she thought, "much of our
own significance is unknown to us, being given to us by
others in awe or pity, and so part of a picture we cannot
see." She had a significance for them; that was to say, in
general—but not now. She knew them well enough to
know that.

"Which of the girls do you think will open the gate?"

"Harris will nip out," Fred told Lilia.

—The letters, how had they come into the house?
Sent back to Guy, why? A breaking-off, a reproach, a
revengeful act? Or had she died, leaving somebody else
to take speaking action? Had they returned here among
Guy's things after Guy's death? Or had he, alive, on one
of his leaves here, wandering with the husks of them in

his hand, seeking their right grave, bitterly or poetically buried them in the cerements of some other expired summer, the muslin of the dress? Or hoarded them, with their charge of love, against such a winter as, for all he knew, he might have to live to see? Then, why not her letters, why his own? Better recall how it felt to love; to have been loved means a little less. Nor had they been buried, but lightly hidden—hidden to be found. Found as they might be found by a seeking girl on an idle evening.

Or, after he had been killed, while Montefort more or less stood empty, had there unknown been a comer to the place, letters in her hand? No knowing what anybody will do—such as make a journey simply to set eyes upon an obelisk, a bit of river, a rock looking into a pool as it did in letters; to see, by seeing these in reality, that so far at least as *these* went he had been true with her; or to behold them simply for his sake? Pleading or buying her way into his house, looking into his rooms, out of his windows—what was to stop her? Stacked in the attics, to wait forever, she would find his familiar things which, having come home without him, unbearably said: "So this is the end." So from that she fled—thrusting the letters under the lid of a trunk to lie stifled there with a muslin woman; for, as she would have heard, there had been Lilia. . . . Nothing so foolish could be impossible: wherever one looks twice, there is some mystery. However the letters had come into the house, they were now gone.

So was the van. Satisfaction yet disappointment (for something else might have happened at the last moment) spread slowly over the watching faces, announcing that it was out of view. So that was that. Fred, who'd already looked at his watch, must now be off to get on with something: he vanished forthwith into the house, taking a cut through the hall to the yard door. Lilia began: "Well, I may as well . . ." sighed, and alternately smoothed her forearms, drawing out the action as long as possible. "What were *you* intending to do, Antonia?" she asked, as though for aid.

"I don't know.—Or do you mean, now?"

"Well, this afternoon.—Oh, I didn't mean in the future!"

"And why not?" asked Antonia, absently scanning the face of Montefort.

"Look," said Lilia, pointing, "you've left your cup on the grass!"

Antonia went back and picked up the cup. "But for the future," she said, "we'd have nothing left."

THE VAN bounded along smoothly, at a rate appropriate to its size—the obelisk dropped from view, leaving the skyline to be one continuous flowing change, and the road after the early miles began to untrammel itself from hedges, so that space pastorally widened on either hand. Banks were innocent-blue with scabious, whole fields chalky with moon-daisies, and trees, hiding one knew not what, made islands. Arched stone bridges swooped with the van across rivers as unexpected as they were small—and though for some way yet to the girls' eyes nothing intrinsically was new or failed to resemble something they'd seen before, the unmistakable breath of the unknown came to meet them ever more strongly, and pure strangeness lay over the opening country. Glimpses, snatched from them half-seen, caused them this way or that way to duck their heads: they were, as they could not help showing, unused to touring—or, in Jane's case, at any rate in Ireland: when in favour, she'd been to the sea with Antonia, but that, from Montefort, had been almost all. Today, their course lay inland: Harris was single-mindedly heading north-west, towards a defile through the range of mountains dividing this corner of County Cork from the large lush lakelike County Limerick plain.

Nor, enlarged by the clarity of today, did the mountains hesitate to come closer: before one knew, they were crowding around the van, which traced its nonchalant course between them. At the outset, Harris's attitude had been uncertain. The order along the front seat was as follows: himself, Maud, the non-dimensional

Gay David, and Jane with an elbow out of a window.
Something in the set-up was clearly more than he'd bar-
gained for: consequently, all to be said of Harris for
some time was that he drove. Not till they were into the
scenery did he volunteer that nothing was like Switzerland.

"No," agreed Jane, "I suppose not."

"Or where this Mr. Richard's coming from—Colorado."

"Oh?"

"So I understand."

"You understand he's coming from Colorado, or that
Colorado is as unlike as Switzerland?"

"Never said anything of that sort," said Harris, vex-
edly braking to avoid a goat. "For one thing, Switzerland's full of snow."

"*I* could have told you that," said Maud, who had
been remarkably silent so far. "What on earth's he doing
in Colorado?"

Jane, also interested, lent ear; but Harris no more
than gave out: "Ranching, they principally do there;
but I couldn't tell you."

"Or why isn't he staying in Colorado?" pursued
Maud.

"Ask me another," said Harris sternly. "And what
have you got there with you—a pixie, eh?"

For Maud's duality as a passenger became oppressive

—sidelong communication, other than with her sister, had been going on, off and on and more on than off, ever since the van had turned out of Montefort. Each time the child slid down on the seat she'd seemed to be dragging with her another entity, whom she kept down with her in a grapple; and each time she'd reared herself up again she'd done so with an oblique bullying hoist, forcing whatever it might be to sit still more erect, take still more furious notice than she had decided to do herself. She and her familiar would have been matched but that Maud just always came out on top. This preoccupation with Gay David, whose chastening if mindbroadening outing the afternoon evidently was, had relieved the others of much of Maud, at least up to now; but it rattled Harris, particularly up here in the mountains. He had scented something fishy about this trip when the diversion to Montefort had been ordered, though what her ladyship might be up to this time was of little interest to him. But unnatural occupancy of his van he had not foreseen, nor would he stand for it. "Who said you were to, anyway?" he said nastily.

"Oh, Harris," Jane interposed, bored, "don't go on like that! That's only Maud's elemental."

"Elemental what?" said the chauffeur.

"To keep her happy," the elder sister said. "Anyone must have somebody, don't you find?"

"*I* never found it necessary," said Harris.

"Happy!" said Maud bitterly. "With this fat foul fiend? *Grrrrr!*"

"Well, leave him alone," said Jane; then gave herself to the last of the mountain landscape, for they now were winding downhill towards the flat; then yawned, like Peregrine or her father, then observed: "It does seem thousands of miles to come."

Harris remarked: "And brought here for nothing."

Jane considered Harris went too far, till he surprised her very much by explaining: "His mother was to have been at the castle; that was to have been the idea. But now she's cancelled."

"But I didn't know that he had a mother."

Harris nodded. "Lifelong friend of her ladyship's, until recently. Mrs. Priam, her name was."

"Isn't it now?"

"Shan't be seeing much more of *her*, I suppose. Anyway, whatever it was, she's cancelled. So now what's he going to do?"

Jane, though uncertainly, said she could not imagine.

"Not much for him to do at the castle, is there?" Harris continued. "Stuck it out last time he and his mother was here because of the fishing; but look what the fishing's like this year. No, you can be a good son once too often."

"But her ladyship—" Jane broke off, confused.

"I should know," Harris went on, "I was a good son,

up to any reasonable point. Well, they won't get *him* off another plane again in a hurry, when you think how he could have gone through to London."

"What's he like?" said Jane.

"He's all right."

Jane felt all at sea. "Well, Harris, this should at least be a lucky day for *you*," she at length said, with a deferential glance at the omen wilting in his buttonhole. Harris cleared his throat and said: "Well, you might have thought so."

The van broached the Limerick plain: bowling along the straight, straight road, it grew smaller under so much sky. For the girls there was little to look at other than much that was much the same—this, some of the richest land in Ireland, was showing the same anxiety as their land at home; but the climax of the expectation seemed to be over, the obdurate cloud-ceiling still saying nothing. There was, though still there were daisies, a smell of dust. The air, of which the flatness allowed for much, seemed if anything harder than the land— birds as though labouring flew through it, under the influence of the hush, and one could imagine with what effort anything larger than a bird must have to continue to forge its way; though at the altitude out of sight at which the airliner anxiously must be hastening in order to converge upon the van at the given time, at the given spot, all might be otherwise—one could not say. The

passengers, unable to see down, might all the same be
looking down, just as Jane, unable to see up, was looking up—her forehead out of the window. Maud might
not have been beside her; and as for Harris, he drove on,
on, on, in what seemed a stern sleep.

There was an ebb of the senses, during the plain.

But here came Limerick city, which was something;
indeed—as the suburbs gave place to Georgian exten-
sive streets, shops and infatuated shoppers—much. "Oh,
look," cried Jane, "there's even an officer in uniform!"

"Irish army," said Harris, able to see anything without looking.

"And what's the matter with that?" Maud wanted to
know, rightly incensed.

"Not when you've been in the *Army*," said Harris,
"see?" He pulled up at lights, which gave them a moment: Jane studied the reflection of the van in the suf-
ficient window of an emporium—herself, in it, in town,
in an impotent jam of halted traffic, caught; and she saw
why she could not go back to London, to the girls' resi-
dential club where Antonia put her when at a loss, to
the room-mate who was the sort of bore who was not a
virgin. "Wonder what more's been happening to *her?*"
she thought, hoping never to have to know. The lights
changed; the van slid forward across the main street towards the open river ahead; the closure on Jane lightened and was gone—having been due probably to the

businesslike darkness of the Limerick houses **at that** point. *"We're* a military family," she told Harris, who restricted himself to crossing the river bridge among many and reckless bicycles; while Maud, impressed, stared up then down the Shannon. "Or rather, we were."

Over the bridge, they were into the County Clare, which, due to end in a mad void utter rocky declivity to the West, had nothing to show so far but substantial villas. "What, died out, have you?" asked Harris idly, overshooting a bus.

Maud said: "Good gracious, no!"

"There are no more men, Maud," Jane admitted, though letting her eye be caught by a profusion of roses in one of the gardens.

"What d'you call your father?" asked Harris, shocked.

"No more to come, I mean."

"Well, never say die," he said, though not with the matter deeply at heart. Sucking in a cheek on the sisters' side, he conveyed his wish to be bothered by them no more, his exclusive purpose from now on being to reach the airport; and Jane, as though to aid him by concentration, sat for some time leaning a little forward, brow to the road like a beautiful figurehead's. Out petered the villas with their stories. Straight was the road again, with wooded green hills engraved along at a distance to its right, giving there a niche for a nameless mansion, there a backdrop to a ruinous tower: patches of rushes in the fields proclaimed that this was a marshy watershed, across which ran the highway bare as a dyke. What was amazing was that the world could change so fast—where they had been, where was it now? And, still more, what was to come? Air as it tore by the open windows entered and lifted the speeding van, and this was in a sort of crescendo, making Jane's hands clasp and reclasp.

Maud stirred. "Are we late for the aeroplane?"

"*I* don't know," said her sister, with an uncaring laugh. "Are we, or aren't we?" she put it to Harris.

"*You* don't have to worry," was all he elected to let them know.

"But I want," said Maud, "to see it come down."

"I should rather like to," said Jane also.

"Well, you will," he said, "if that's all you want. That plane's got to come over the Atlantic—what d'you expect it to be, then: before time? Also I've known them go round and round."

"Round and round what?"

"Till they get the come-on from the control."

"Then why are we hurrying?" asked Maud, still not altogether easy in mind.

"Because *I* like to be on time, see?" said Harris, showing a dangerous eye.

"Oh, shut up, Maud," interceded Jane.

Water skeined the landscape. The Shannon River,

lost since Limerick city, was drawing nearer to name the airport, and a tributary quickened its way towards it. Over the tributary, a humpbacked bridge, over which on guard stood up a castle like Shalott—willows whitened, aspens quivered; and how far did the top turrets see? The van whisked over the bridge, into a shaded swastika-angled section of the road due soon to go on without them to Galway, for soon would be coming the Turn Off. Subdued by the trees and by the narrowed intensity of this all-but-last phase, both girls said nothing. When the Turn Off did come, it was a vast taut cemented causeway, special, polished-looking like solidified water: all else stood back from it in awe, for it looked like the future and for some was. Yet this the Latterly van was now travelling in an accustomed way. "How do you beware of low-flying aircraft?" Maud asked, reading a warning notice.

"Time enough to see when the time comes."

Miles of runway were sunk in this coarse grass. The magnetic little buildings of the great airport, sky-flattened, were appearing to circle, shifting from point to point like a hard mirage as the causeway turned—they were all but there, and now here they were. Harris parked the van. The sisters, one on each side of him, walked past the introductory flowerbeds and flagpoles, instinctively trying to hold their heads as though they had often been here before. Knowledgeably pulling at a succession of glassy doors, he caused the party to enter: here was a place of indoor settees, ashtrays, and low tables, not like a room but like nothing else. One whole wall, however, was a window, outside which an airliner was to be seen sitting upon its tail; the sight of that hit them in the eye, causing Maud to say: "*Well*—?" to Harris, with bitter and unutterable reproach.

"Well, what's the matter with that? It's a K.L.M.; it's got as much right to the place as you have.—This is where you wait, though," he told Jane.

"Oh, yes, Harris.—For how long?"

"Till it's called," he said, and went off somewhere.

Maud went off to where one could bid for chocolate and dishevel numbers of magazines.

Jane sat down on the ledge of the vast window. Her back was to space: she knew it was there, so did not turn round, preferring for some reason to examine twists of paper dropped into an ashtray by someone gone. Nothing is so simple as you hope; the girl did not know what to do now—"Oh, yes," she thought, "I *am* doing something, I am waiting"; but reason told her that waiting is not a thing you do. A wait is something being done to you. She thought of her mother in the railway station, but in that case the train had gone: you do not wait for what has already happened. But were there not those who said that everything *has* already happened, and that one's lookings-forward are really memories? However, the girl could not go into that; she did not know— her blazer being across her knee, she ran a finger slowly

along a stripe, for the sake of seeing anything move
in this dead standstill. Rubber-muted silence would
have surrounded her, but that far-off doors sucking
open and shut from time to time fanned through de-
grees of voices: this part of the airport was to be felt
to consist of unechoing corridors, barricades, and at-
trition—she wondered where "the control" was, and, if
it *was* a control, what it could do. A glassed-in bar was
in view from here, and at it a couple on the verge of
goodbye were sitting drinking in twisted silence; and in
fact the conditioned air in here was used up, staled by
partings and meetings, heartbreaking last moments and
eager first ones not to be lived up to in after life, as by
the dust which was never quite to be vacuum-cleaned
from the settees and chairs.—The girl made one of her
beautiful blind impatient movements, perhaps the last.

For the amplifier coughed and began to talk. It spoke
first in Irish; then, having set up enough suspense, in
the other tongue repeated a company's announcement
of the arrival of one of its flights. Maud came by, eating,
saying: *"Aren't* you coming out?" Jane put on her blazer
and followed Maud out through a glass door. This must
be it; for in the railed enclosure with other onlookers
Harris had reappeared.

The scattering of people were looking up. And the
sky, as though reminded of something else, began at
this moment to let fall far-apart tepid drops, each so surprising as it splashed on to cuff, forehead, or eyelid, as to

seem larger than it was; each too individual and mo-
mentous to be rain. The drops, one could imagine,
could be heard; and they distracted attention from any
diluted humming above the cloud-ceiling; or did so till
this began to concentrate into a pinpoint and pierce
through. The sound went on, like pressure upon a nerve,
and the plane came sifting through into visibility: one
watched its hesitating descent to such, alas, a remote
part of the airport that, landing, it dropped again out of
view. It remedied this by coming taxiing endlessly, endlessly inward along the runways, first at one angle, then
at another, and so absurd was its progress in this manner,
one could have wept. "I did not think much of that,"
said Maud, as the thing gave a final tremble and drew
up, more or less opposite them.

Steps and an airport official went out to meet it: at
the conclusion of the formalities the passengers began
to descend—glazed, dazed, indifferent to the earth they
were to know for so short a time, they came past the
watchers one by one. They were interminable: then
came a pause. Maud, having scanned each from top to
toe, balancing on her stomach upon the rail, remarked:
"That seems to be all." Jane, who throughout had been
watching Harris's face for any flicker of recognition,
said: "Then he probably hasn't come."

"Not necessarily," said Harris. "They let the transit
passengers off first."

"Why?"

"Because this is where he gets off."

"Something's still going on inside that aeroplane," said Maud. An individual trailing a carried overcoat and inexpertly holding a gift parcel, forgotten, gone back to his seat for, and recovered, which had prolonged fare-wells to the air hostess, head-stooped under the door and all but pitched himself down the steps. The descent was made with a look of ease at being at large again. Harris immediately turned away, to seek for a more advantaged position from which to step forward touching his cap.

Richard Priam's gait marked him as not being a transit passenger. His glance ran over the thin crowd, as he slowed down past it, not so much expectantly as with a readiness to be expected, an eagerness to smile could he find cause. He spotted Harris in time to see Harris go; next the gap remained a girl in a blazer, collar up as though she expected the skies to fall, gold hair bent outward over the collar. She seemed, too, in the act of turning away, of indeed fleeing, but had not yet done so. She wore the air of someone who cannot help know-ing she must be recognized; her not yet willing but lovely gaze rested, accordingly, upon nothing; or rather upon a point in the diminishing nothingness between him and her.

He swerved nearer the rail, crying "Hullo!" as though to somebody behind her. There was, as she knew, no one. Their eyes met.

They no sooner looked but they loved.

A NOTE ON THE TYPE

THE TEXT of this book has been set on the Linotype in a type-face called Baskerville. The face is a facsimile reproduction of type cast from molds made for John Baskerville (1706–75) from his designs. The punches for the revived Linotype Baskerville were cut under the supervision of the English printer George W. Jones. John Baskerville's original face was one of the forerunners of the type-style known as "modern face" to printers: a "modern" of the period A.D. 1800.

The book was composed, printed, and bound by KINGSPORT PRESS, INC., Kingsport, Tenn.

Typography and binding design by GEORGE SALTER